Joan Weir

Stoddart Kids

TORONTO • NEW YORK

*We gratefully acknowledge the Canada Council for the Arts
and the Ontario Arts Council for their support of our
publishing program.*

Published in Canada in 1998 by
Stoddart Kids,
a division of Stoddart Publishing Co. Limited
34 Lesmill Road
Toronto, Canada M3B 2T6
Tel. (416) 445-3333   Fax (416) 445-5967
E-mail Customer.Service@ccmailgw.genpub.com

Published in the United States in 1999 by
Stoddart Kids,
a division of Stoddart Publishing Co. Limited
180 Varick Street, 9th Floor,
New York, New York 10014
Toll free 1-800-805-1083
E-mail gdsinc@genpub.com

Distributed in Canada by
General Distribution Services
325 Humber College Blvd.,
Toronto, Canada M9W 7C3
Tel. (416) 213-1919   Fax (416) 213-1917
E-mail Customer.Service@ccmailgw.genpub.com

Distributed in the United States by
General Distribution Services
85 River Rock Drive, Suite 202
Buffalo, New York 14207
Toll free 1-800-805-1083
E-mail gdsinc@genpub.com

Canadian Cataloguing in Publication Data

Weir, Joan, 1928–
The brideship

ISBN 0-7736-7474-8

I. Title.

PS8595.E48B65 1998   jC813'.54   C98-930515-5
PZ7.W44Br 1998

Cover Design: Tannice Goddard
Cover Illustration: David Craig
Text Design: Kinetics Design & Illustration

Printed and bound in Canada

*For my sister Bobbie, for her love and
unfailing encouragement*

*For Orm as always and for
Kathryn Edwards with affection and thanks*

Acknowledgement

The poem in this story, "You'll not be with me when the spring is here" was inspired by "A Memory," written in the early 1920s by Canadian poet Francis J. Sherman.

Chapter 1

"How many girls will you require?" Matron's coarse voice carried clearly into the orphanage hallway.

Sarah's polishing cloth stopped in mid-air. She'd been forbidden dinner for the past two nights and put to work polishing the huge brass candlesticks on the entranceway table because Matron had caught her reading in bed. In Matron's opinion, no girl should be allowed to read, in bed or out, certainly not a girl orphan. Reading was an invitation to trouble for it encouraged independence and disobedience.

Admitting to herself that Matron was probably right, Sarah pushed back the unruly strands of long dark hair that, as usual, had refused to stay under her work cap, and strained to listen.

"Four dozen," a voice answered.

It was a man's voice. Men never came to the orphanage!

"We're looking," the voice continued, "for girls who are. . ."

"Fresh perch! Fresh perch 'n cockles!" The cry of a fish peddler on the street outside smothered the quiet voice in the office.

Impatiently Sarah moved closer. What kind of girls was he looking for?

". . . think it would be better if you did not explain too much about the trip ahead of time."

"Not tell them where they are going?"

"No, or what their job is . . ."

Again the voice in the office was smothered, this time by the sound of a carriage rumbling by outside.

". . . going with them yourself, Mr. Brown?" Matron was asking.

"No. I will see them off, but I'm needed here. However, the man who will go in my place has been recommended by a well-respected clergyman. He'll take good care of the girls and make sure they are well-schooled in their duties."

"Are you sure I shouldn't tell them what those duties are to be?"

"Not till they are on their way. It might create too much excitement, or some of them might be unduly anxious."

What sort of job could be too exciting or shouldn't be talked about? Forgetting that she was supposed to be working, Sarah clutched up the ankle-length skirt of her gingham uniform and darted across the hall. She was glad

Matron's opinions about propriety forced her to keep the door open when she had a male visitor.

"Who's there?" Matron's sharp voice demanded from inside the office.

In her haste, Sarah had forgotten more than just the brass she was supposed to be polishing. She'd forgotten how much noise flatsoled orphanage boots make on a bare wood floor. Stepping out of the ill–fitting boots, she swept them up, then raced across the open hall to the safety of the shadowed corner. Pressing tight against the wall, she prayed her stomach wouldn't choose that minute to announce it had missed two dinners.

Matron's stiff angular figure appeared in the office doorway. For a moment she stood listening, then moved back out of sight. "Forgive me, Mr. Brown. I thought someone was there. What were you saying?"

Sarah let her held breath out in a long sigh. Relief at not having been caught restored her courage. What was being planned, she wondered? Nothing this exciting had happened at the orphanage during all the months she and Maud had been here. Again she moved closer to the partly open door, but this time she tested each step before putting her weight down. Stocking feet might make no sound but boards could creak. If Matron caught her eavesdropping the punishment wouldn't be just missed suppers and brass polishing. It would include a whipping as well.

She shivered, but not at the memory of the

welts she'd seen left by Matron's whippings. She shivered because the rough wood floor was cold where it pressed against her feet through the holes in her stockings. Maybe she really should follow her cousin Maud's advice and mend them, she mused. But then how often did she go in stocking feet on the bare wood floor?

A few steps closer and she could again hear the voices.

". . . We'll send four dozen girls to start with," the male voice was saying, "then a great many more if this first group is well received."

"I assume you'll want girls who are as obedient and attractive as possible."

Matron's smug tone made Sarah bristle. Why were girls judged only on looks and behavior, as if they had no value except to please men? She'd promised herself when Momma died that she'd never let that happen to her.

"But not timid."

"The trip could be dangerous?"

"Possibly. Also long and uncomfortable."

"Then I hope the man who is going with them is understanding." Matron's frown sounded in her voice.

"I haven't met him yet," Mr. Brown admitted. "I understand he is hoping to become a minister himself and sees this as a way to prove his ability. His married sister will be traveling with them as well, so the girls will be in good hands."

Sarah's heart was racing. This was exactly the sort of opportunity she'd longed for ever since she'd come to the orphanage — a chance to prove what she could do in some worthwhile job. The man said four dozen girls would be going. If only she could be one of them.

Eager to catch a glimpse of Matron's visitor, she inched closer to the partly open door. Then she almost gave her presence away with a gasp of surprise, for the man in Matron's office looked just like Uncle Tor, the same kind, laughing eyes, the same gleaming white clerical collar, the same oxford grey suit.

Tears welled up hot behind Sarah's eyelids. Uncle Tor had been Momma's brother. After Momma had got so sick, Sarah had lived with Uncle Tor and her cousin Maud. They'd wanted Momma to come and live with them too so they could look after her, but she had refused. Papa might come back, she'd said. She must be there waiting.

Sarah had begged Momma to change her mind. Papa wasn't coming back — he'd forgotten all about them. "Please, Momma. I want to be with you."

Momma's arms had closed around her and held her tight. "It's only for a little while, Sarah. As soon as the warm weather comes I'll be well again, then I'll bring you back here to live with me."

Sarah had never seen her again, for though the warm weather had come, Momma hadn't lived to see it.

That had been five years ago. Early in this spring of 1862 Uncle Tor had died too. That was when Sarah and her cousin Maud had been sent to the orphanage.

"You say you don't want girls who are timid," Matron was saying. "Then can I include a girl who tends to be rather independent? Not pushy or defiant," she added quickly as if afraid her visitor might say no.

"I don't mind her being independent as long as it doesn't prevent her carrying out her role."

Sarah envied the unnamed girl. If only she could change places, for she was independent too. Momma had insisted she learn to be, though she'd often wondered why, for Momma hadn't been independent at all.

"How old is this girl you're thinking of including?"

"Not quite sixteen. I had arranged to have her apprenticed in the mills. She was to start at the end of this month. But if I could send her with you instead it would remove the possibility of any criticism."

"Criticism?"

"People might feel I should have tried to find something more suitable for her. Her uncle was a well-respected clergyman."

Matron was talking about her! The excitement Sarah had been feeling changed to horror. Matron had been planning to send her to the mills — sixteen-hour work days — bread and porridge to eat — a mat somewhere for sleeping —

"Include her by all means."

"Her older cousin is also at the orphanage." Matron let the words hang on the air in an unasked question.

"Send them both if you wish."

With obvious relief, Matron rubbed the palms of her hands down the sides of her thick mauve skirt. "It would be a great help," she admitted. "Girls who have been educated tend to stir up trouble in an institution like this. You'd think any intelligent man would realize that teaching girls to read and question just fills their heads with impractical dreams."

"Does it indeed?" The clergyman's voice was dry.

Sarah's delighted glance flew to his face. She liked this man who looked like Uncle Tor and who thought girls had a right to be educated and make something of themselves.

If Matron caught the dryness in her visitor's tone she gave no sign. "When are the girls to go?"

"June 7th."

"That's in ten days."

"Is it too soon?"

"No. I'll have them ready."

It wasn't safe to stay listening any longer. Sarah still hadn't found out where they were going or for what purpose, but who cared? All that mattered was that she wasn't to be apprenticed in the mills. Instead she was to be included in some exciting adventure. Whatever job they gave her, no matter how hard it might be, she'd carry it through successfully. And she wouldn't complain even if the trip was lonely and dangerous. As long as Maud was going too, there was nothing to fear.

Still in her stocking feet with her heavy orphanage boots clutched in one hand, Sarah set off to find her cousin and tell her the news.

Chapter 2

Maud was in the damp basement kitchen scraping the potatoes that would form the major part of the girls' supper.

"I've been looking everywhere for you!" Sarah exclaimed, catapulting down the stairs.

The rhythm of Maud's potato scraping didn't falter, but a twinkle came into her dark eyes. "Don't tell me. Let me guess. You're in trouble again, Saree."

"No, I'm not! At least, maybe I am — but — oh, I've so much to tell you!"

"First," Maud said, nodding at the boots in Sarah's hand, "put those back on before Matron catches you."

"In a minute."

Sarah plunged into her recital. When she reached the part about Matron intending to apprentice her in the mills, Maud looked as if she was going to interrupt, but Sarah gave her no chance. She rushed on, running the words together. "And you can come too," she finished breathlessly. "The clergyman said so."

Whatever Maud had been going to say about the mills was forgotten. The smile faded from her eyes. "Did the clergyman say it was certain I was to go?"

"No, but he said you could."

Maud pushed back some strands of damp hair from her forehead and resumed her potato scraping.

"It's our chance to prove we can make our own way in the world, Maud! It's what we've been waiting for — to prove we can be independent!"

Maud continued to concentrate on the potatoes. "Where will this group of girls be going?"

Sarah shifted uncomfortably on the damp scullery floor. The wooden hall upstairs had been warm compared with these stones. Maybe Maud was right — maybe she should put her boots on. "It doesn't matter where we're going. Once we prove we can do this job, all sorts of opportunities will open up."

Maud's expression remained inscrutable. "When the girls finish whatever job they're to do, will they come back here?"

"Of course." Even as Sarah spoke she realized no one had actually said that, but she didn't bother to correct herself. It was obviously what was intended. "That's why it's so exciting. The clergyman said the job was important and we'd be really welcome when we got there. We're to leave in ten days."

Maud had started on a fresh potato, but now she dropped it in the sink together with the scraping knife and caught Sarah's hand. "Ten — No, Saree! Not when we don't know anything about where we would be going or for what purpose. It's too much of a risk."

Impatiently Sarah pulled her hand free. "Who minds risks? Don't you see, Maud? We can make this a wonderful adventure! Anyway," she added practically, "if Matron decides we're to go she won't change her plans because of what we want."

"She will if I speak to her and explain about Harley."

Sarah turned away. When would Maud stop dreaming? Of course her cousin was head over heels in love with the handsome student minister at church, but so were half the girls in the orphanage. Granted, Harley beamed every time he saw her, but ministers were supposed to beam at people. That was part of their job. It didn't mean he had any intention of marrying Maud. However, she refused to see that — just as she refused to see that poor student ministers weren't likely to marry girls from orphanages who had no dowry and no connections — not when they might just as easily marry rich ones.

"I'll speak to Matron right after supper," Maud went on, starting again on the potatoes.

"If you do," Sarah returned through lips that

had suddenly gone stiff and cold, "I'll be sent to the mills."

Maud didn't even pause in her peeling. "Not after I explain that as soon as Harley and I are married you'll be coming to live with us."

Quickly Sarah busied herself putting on her boots while she chose her words, for otherwise she was afraid she might say something she'd regret. At last she straightened. "Please, Maud, don't speak to Matron. Please come with me on this trip instead. We'll be back long before you and Harley are ready to get married. This is my chance to make something of my life, and I want to take it. Only I need you to come with me, because . . . I'm . . . I'm scared to go alone."

"I'm scared to go too, Saree."

"Neither of us will be scared if we're together."

The speed of Maud's scraping increased.

"Please, Maud?"

For a moment longer Sarah waited, then in a low voice added, "You promised Uncle Tor."

The moment the words were spoken Sarah wanted to call them back, for Maud's cheeks turned chalk white. Why hadn't she kept quiet? True, when Uncle Tor was dying he'd asked Maud to promise to look after Sarah, but Maud had kept that promise. She'd done everything she could to smooth the way for her young cousin. Even now when she talked of marrying Harley she insisted that Sarah would live with them. "Maud, I take it back! You've kept your promise. You don't have to do anything more!"

Maud continued to concentrate on the potatoes but her hands were shaking so badly the knife refused to work.

Sarah felt sick inside. Her cousin wasn't strong. A trip like this might be too much for her. When they'd lived at Uncle Tor's it had always been Maud who suffered most when a cold or the flu swept through the house. Sarah should never have mentioned Maud's promise. Now her cousin would feel she had to go, no matter how much she dreaded it.

Unless this trip turned out to be the wonderful adventure Sarah was sure it would — then there would be nothing for Maud to dread.

The thought came out of nowhere, and as it did Sarah's panic faded. True, Maud wasn't looking forward to the trip at the moment, but as soon as it started she'd change her mind. Before they'd been underway even a day, Maud would be glad she'd come.

Chapter 3

As supper finished that evening, Matron rose to her feet. Dabbing at her lips with the napkin that she alone had been provided with, she glanced over the rows of girls sitting in crowded silence at the bare wood tables in front of her.

"Four dozen of you have been selected for a special honor," she announced in brisk, businesslike tones. "You will be leaving the orphanage in a little over a week."

"Leaving for where?" voices wondered in excited undertones.

"You will be told the details of the trip later. Meantime, the names of those who have been selected are on a list on the notice board in the hall. After supper you can check to see if you are included."

"Cor, wudn't it be somethin' to get sent some-place away from 'ere?" whispered a voice.

Sarah nodded, but now that the moment had come she was terrified. What if she and Maud weren't on the list after all? What if Matron had changed her mind?

"'Ow does she expect us to know if we're on 'er list," the same voice continued, "if she don't read it out to us?"

Sarah looked at the wiry, light-haired girl beside her. "I'll look for your name," she promised. She didn't blame Lizzie for being annoyed. Matron knew most of the girls had never had a chance to learn to read.

Her own supper finished, Matron got to her feet, flounced out her heavy skirts, then moved through the crowd of tables toward the door.

The girls sat motionless while her footsteps echoed across the uncarpeted hall and her office door closed. Then the dining hall burst into life.

Sarah and Lizzie had been seated at the table farthest from the exit. By the time they reached the hallway, a mass of gingham-clad figures stood between them and the notice board, but Lizzie wriggled through. Next moment she was right at the front, peering up at the names on Matron's list with a puzzled expression on her thin face. Standing beside her, peering equally intently, was Arabella, in Sarah's opinion one of the prettiest girls in the orphanage.

Sarah made no move to join them. She was afraid to look.

"When you g–g–go to check your name, would

you see if m–m–mine is there too?" asked a soft, slow voice at Sarah's shoulder. "I'm hoping it won't be."

Sarah turned in surprise to the large, homey–looking girl beside her. "You mean you don't want to go?"

Fanny shook her head. "Because of me m–m–mum." Her voice was slow and deliberate in an attempt to control the stutter. "When they sent m–m–me to the orphanage they sent her to the w–w–workhouse. Now she's took sick. Real b–b–bad. She needs me to come visit."

"But Matron never lets anyone leave the orphanage, no matter who's sick."

"She p–p–promised she'd try to arrange it."

"Then she won't have put you on the list."

"Just the same, w–w–will you check?"

Sarah nodded. By now the crowd in front of the notice board had started to thin. It was impossible to hang back any longer. She had no choice but to move forward. Half a dozen steps and she was close enough to see the names. She scanned the list, but there was no sign of Maud's name or hers. Struggling to stay calm, she started again at the top.

She was so tense and the crowd of girls around the notice board was so tight that her head began to spin. She felt the floor rushing toward her.

"Put yer 'ead between yer knees," a voice said from what seemed a long way off. Next second, Sarah felt someone's hand on her back, dou-bling her over.

Her head steadied.

"Wos you faintin' 'cos yer going or 'cos yer not?" Lizzie asked.

"Because I can't find our names." Again Sarah's panic started to rise. If they weren't on Matron's list it meant she'd be sent to the mills!

Just as she was sure that was her fate she found her name and Maud's scrawled in Matron's awkward handwriting in the middle of the column. With a rush of relief, she turned. "It's all right, Maud!" she called across the room to her cousin. "Our names are here!"

The color drained from Maud's cheeks.

"My name's there too," Lizzie said excitedly. She pointed near the top of the list. "That 'as to be me. Ain't nobody else 'as them squiggly Zs in their name."

Sarah was staring after Maud.

"Did you see m–m–my name?" Fanny asked.

Sarah had been so concerned about herself and her cousin that she'd forgotten her promise to Fanny. Quickly she turned and scanned the list again. She'd almost reached the bottom and was just about to tell Fanny it was all right — that she wasn't included — when her eyes caught the last name. *Fanny Buchanan.*

"Oh, Fanny, yes!" she said in a tight voice.

Fanny's face crumpled. Two large tears formed in her eyes and spilled in slow motion down her cheeks. "When I don't come M–M–Mum will think I don't c–c–care." Brushing at her eyes with the back of one work-roughened hand, she turned and started back across the hall toward the girls' quarters.

"Cor," said Lizzie.

Sarah went funny inside. For her tenth birthday Uncle Tor had given her a black mongrel puppy. She'd called him Sooter. His feet had been too big, his tail too long, and one ear never seemed to learn how to stand up properly, but from the moment he arrived Sarah's world was different. Every day he'd wait while she finished her lessons and her chores, then they'd escape into the fields. Sometimes Sarah would hide on him. It took only moments for him to find her, but it could have been hours the way he wriggled all over and crinkled his eyes with happiness.

The day she and Maud were taken away to the orphanage Sooter had begged to go too. He thought he must have done something wrong and he pleaded with her to forgive him. Sarah tried to explain — to tell him goodbye — to tell him she loved him — but he was only a dog and he didn't understand.

The look in Fanny's eyes was the same as that look in Sooter's. "It must be a mistake, Fanny! Matron must have forgotten about your mum. Go and speak to her —"

If Fanny heard she gave no sign.

Chapter 4

"I don't care if we're goin' to the North Pole, just so long as we go quick," Lizzie told Sarah nine days later as they stood with the rest of the orphanage girls in the early morning cold. All were dressed alike in ankle-length gingham uniforms, dark bonnets and ugly orphanage boots, and all except Lizzie wore dark woven shawls around their shoulders.

Lizzie must have packed hers away in her bag, Sarah decided. She probably didn't want to start this adventure wearing anything so drab and old-fashioned. Sarah wished she'd had the courage to do the same, but she'd been too cold. She was still cold — even with her shawl.

Lizzie, without one, was shivering noticeably. "I Dare you to get into one of them cosylookin' carriages," she challenged, nodding toward six horse-drawn carriages waiting by the side of the road.

Sarah glanced up. "All right. Only, you go first."

"Saree!" Maud protested.

Sarah ignored her cousin. She held Lizzie's gaze firmly and prayed she would take back the challenge, for they both knew what would happen if they moved even a step closer to those carriages before Matron gave permission. But if Lizzie held firm, Sarah would have to as well. A person couldn't refuse a Dare.

For another endless moment the gleam in Lizzie's green eyes continued to challenge, then her face relaxed into a grin. With a resigned sigh, she glanced briefly at Matron then raised her eyes skyward.

Letting out the breath she'd been holding, Sarah giggled.

"Sareee!"

"We were only fooling," Sarah told her cousin, then quickly changed the subject. "Where could they be sending us that we need new boots?" She deliberately slid her feet from side to side in her new ones which were fully two sizes too wide. At least they didn't have holes. For the first time in months she could stand on the wet cobblestones and not have her coarse worsted stockings turn mushy with damp. "We must be going somewhere special for them to give us both new boots and these." She nodded toward the small blue carpetbags lying at each girl's feet.

Maud's displeasure faded at the mention of the bags.

Lizzie picked hers up. She ran her hands over it lovingly. "Cor. Ain't these somethin'?"

The bags had been given out just before the girls had left the orphanage, and excitement still lit their faces. Lizzie wasn't the only one who had never owned a bag of her own before.

Each bag contained a cup, bowl, spoon, and the basic articles of clothing the girls would need in addition to the clothes they wore — a second cotton shift laundered to a dull grey color; a second pair of coarse cotton underdrawers that extended below the knee and were fastened at the waist with a drawstring cord; a second pair of thick worsted stockings; a bibtopped apron with a large front pocket and straps that went over the shoulders; and a wellworn "second–best" uniform.

Into the bags as well the girls had tucked their few personal possessions. Maud had put in writing paper and pencils so she could write to Harley, and four leather-bound books. Three had been Uncle Tor's; the fourth Harley had given her that morning. It contained a collection of his poems.

Deep in the bottom of her own bag, Sarah had hidden Penelope. Momma had made the doll for her after Papa left. "To brighten the dark places and listen to dreams," Momma had said.

Sarah had an idea Momma knew all about dark places and dreams that no one else would listen to.

"Look at that!" Lizzie's voice broke into Sarah's thoughts. She was pointing to an unattended carpetbag lying at the edge of the pavement. "People shudn't leave their things lyin' about."

Before Sarah realized what she was planning, Lizzie had slipped through the crowd. Next moment she'd reached the bag and picked it up. For a moment it seemed to demand her full attention. Then she caught Sarah's eye and grinned. Setting the bag back down exactly where she'd found it, she returned through the crowd. Her eyes were shining.

"Lizzie! You didn't take something!"

"'Course not." For a moment Lizzie looked offended, then her face relaxed into its customary saucy grin. "There weren't nuffin' in there worth taking. 'Oo needs another pair of them drawers?"

Quickly Sarah turned away so Lizzie wouldn't see her smile, only to find Arabella watching with a smug expression. Had Arabella seen Lizzie pick up that carpetbag? Did she think Lizzie had taken something? Sarah wondered if she should try to explain.

But it was too late to worry about Arabella, for Maud was moving toward them. Maud must have seen Lizzie pick up that other bag too. Sarah braced herself for a lecture, for Maud was convinced that Lizzie was a bad influence and that Sarah shouldn't make a friend of her.

But Maud didn't want to talk about Lizzie after all. Instead she asked Sarah if she could see any sign of the clergyman who had been in Matron's office.

For a moment Sarah was surprised. She'd

forgotten that Maud hadn't seen him. "He's not going with us," she reminded her cousin.

"No, but you said he organized everything, so he'll know when we'll be back." Color crept into Maud's cheeks. "I promised Harley I'd let him know in my first letter."

Several times during the past few days Sarah had felt a renewed pang of guilt. Now she felt one again. Could she have been wrong about Maud and Harley? Might he really be in love with her? First he'd come to say goodbye — then he'd brought Maud a present of a book of his own poetry — now he was arranging for them to write to one another. Might he want to marry her after all? Should Sarah never have urged her cousin to come on this trip?

She pushed the worry away. They'd be back within a month or two, she reminded herself. If Harley and Maud were truly in love, two months apart wouldn't matter.

She went back to studying the crowd, hoping the nice clergyman would hurry so Maud could speak to him and so they could get off these wet cobblestones, for she'd been wrong about the boots. Maybe they didn't have holes, but they still let in the wet. It just took longer.

At last a carriage swung into sight, drawn by a team of matched bay horses and driven by the familiar figure in oxford grey.

"There he is," she told Maud in an excited whisper.

Maud watched as the man in grey slowed his horses to a stop, fastened the reins in the holder by the side of the seat, set the carriage brake, then stepped down onto the road.

At almost the same moment, a second carriage pulled up behind the first. A blond-haired man with puffy side whiskers got out.

"That must be the man who will be traveling with us," Sarah said, studying the newcomer. He wasn't wearing a clerical collar and for a moment that made her vaguely uneasy. So did what seemed to be his overly broad smile. But both thoughts were forgotten as another figure stepped down from the carriage — a tall lady in a stylish green traveling dress.

Mr. Brown moved toward the pair, holding out his hand. "We'll be watching with interest to see how you manage this responsibility," he told the younger man.

"I won't let you down, sir. May I introduce my sister, Mrs. Worthing?"

Mr. Brown bowed.

"Go speak to him now," Sarah prompted her cousin.

But before Maud could move, Matron called for attention and ordered the girls to get into the waiting carriages.

For a moment, Maud looked disconcerted, then her expression cleared. "I'll speak to him when we stop. That will probably be better anyway." She followed Sarah to the closest carriage. The horses were whipped up and their vehicle joined the rest, trotting through streets not yet fully awake for the business of the day.

Sarah tried to see where they were going, but

the crush inside the carriage made it impossible to catch more than brief glimpses through the window of the English countryside — sometimes a house — sometimes a patch of green — sometimes some trees.

At last the swaying of the carriage eased. It stopped. The door was opened, letting in the cold and the damp, and the girls were told to alight.

Shivering, Sarah stepped out onto the cobblestones with the others, and for the first time saw the water. To her horror she realized they were standing on the London dock! Next moment, she found herself being marshalled with the others up a gangplank and on board a ship.

The rocking motion under her feet was terrifying. She looked toward Maud for reassurance, but her cousin was just as frightened. Was this what the nice clergyman had meant when he'd said the trip could be dangerous? Where were they being taken? Where was Mr. Brown? Her cousin had to talk to him and explain. She had to tell him about Harley and ask to go back right now. Surely Mr. Brown would let her, for he was a clergyman too. He might even know Harley.

Frantically, Sarah studied the ship. Mr. Brown wasn't on board. At last she located him, still standing on the dock. Perhaps Maud should wait by the gangplank. Then as soon as he —

At that moment, Mr. Brown took off his hat. He made a wide wave with it over his head, then as Sarah watched, he turned and started back the way they'd come.

A moment later the oxford grey suit and the clerical collar were swallowed up by the crowd.

Chapter 5

The forward section of the *S.S.Tynemouth* was fitted with three decks of passenger cabins and a promenade deck. The aft section held the crew's quarters, the engine room and the galley. Amidships on the deck level was a passenger salon. The area underneath this passenger salon was divided into three windowless cargo compartments.

Into the middle one of these cramped and airless compartments, the girls from the orphanage were ushered.

Sarah was still numb from the shock of discovering that Mr. Brown had left before Maud could speak to him. Now the smothering claustrophobia of their quarters settled over her. The air was close and fetid, and it could have been shadowed evening down here — for the tiny, dirt-covered portholes allowed scarcely any daylight to filter through.

"They can't make us stay here!" she told her cousin in a terrified whisper.

Maud took her hand. Her face was pale, but her voice was reassuring. "I know how much you dislike being in closed places, Saree, but this won't be for long. It can't be. There's no provision for us to stay here."

To Sarah's relief she realized Maud was right. Four dozen girls couldn't stay in this cramped cargo space, for there were no chairs or tables, and very little room to move around. She looked more closely at their surroundings.

The compartment space was almost completely taken up with bunks built in triple tiers and fastened securely to the floor. The top bunks would have been usable if they'd had mattresses and blankets, but they didn't. As for the middle and lower bunks, no one could sleep there for they were crowded too closely on top of each other to allow a person to sit up. The only other articles to be seen were three unlit oil lamps hanging from nails hammered into the rafters. With the motion of the ship at anchor the three lamps swung gently back and forth. Quickly Sarah looked away. Wherever they were going she hoped they got there quickly, for even that gentle motion made her stomach turn.

What bothered her most, however, was the smell. Her throat kept closing. She wanted to hold her breath. Could it be from the damp, she wondered, for patches of oily water marked the floorboards, and beads of moisture clung to the walls.

Then for the first time she saw the latrine pails bunched in one corner, four of them — three without lids — and pushed behind them, half a dozen chipped china chamber pots. That's where the smell was coming from. It permeated the closed, airless compartment. Of course Maud was right. They couldn't be made to stay down here very long, but even an hour would be unbearable.

At that moment, two people descended the narrow staircase that led into the crowded compartment — the smiling, blond-haired man with side whiskers whom Mr. Brown had greeted on the dock, and the stylish lady in green who had come with him.

"My name is Mr. Dubonnet," the man told the terrified girls. "And this is my sister, Mrs. Worthing."

The lady beside him didn't even glance up. She seemed more concerned with not letting her skirts touch the oily floor than with saying hello.

"Now, about the bunks," Dubonnet continued, his voice hearty and his smile still in place. "You girls are to use the bottom and middle bunks only. The top ones are reserved for a group of twenty mature governesses who are traveling under my sister's and my chaperonage and who should be joining us at any moment. They, too, are going to the Canadian gold fields."

A terrifying hole opened up somewhere deep inside Sarah. She had been occupied with the impossibility of anyone using the middle and bottom bunks, but that was forgotten as Dubonnet's words sank in. The Canadian gold fields were practically on the other side of the world. How could they be going there? What jobs could there be there for them? It couldn't be true. Her glance flew to her cousin for reassurance, but to her horror she saw her own numb panic reflected in Maud's dark eyes.

"It is a trip most people would envy you for," Mr. Dubonnet went on, still smiling blandly. "Across the Atlantic, around the tip of South America, then up the coastline of South and North America to the Canadian far west."

Forty–eight stunned faces stared back at him.

"Now, about your meals. Your food will be brought to you in weekly allotments. Ration it carefully, for nothing extra will be provided until the week is up."

Lizzie was the first to recover. "We 'aven't to eat down 'ere, 'ave we?" she protested, looking around.

For the first time, Mr. Dubonnet's smile faltered. He located Lizzie in the crowd. For a moment the lines around his mouth seemed to tighten, but when he spoke his voice was as calm and pleasant as ever. "Yes, you will stay down here. You are not to mix with any of the other passengers or even to speak to them. You will keep to your own quarters throughout the voyage except for a period each day when Mrs. Worthing or I will take you up on deck for a walk in the fresh air. It's for your own safety and comfort. Some of the crew or passengers might otherwise try to force their attentions on you."

"I wudn't mind," Lizzie said.

Someone giggled.

Again Mr. Dubonnet's mouth tightened.

"Would you tell us why we are being sent to the Canadian gold fields?" Maud asked in a voice Sarah didn't recognize.

Mr. Dubonnet seemed surprised as he turned to Maud in the crowd. "Haven't they told you?" He looked along the rows of waiting faces and his smile came back. "You're going to be brides for the miners."

Chapter 6

It couldn't be true! This must be some joke. They couldn't be going to the gold fields to be brides for the miners. Mr. Brown had told Matron specifically that they were being sent to carry out some job.

All at once Matron's words surfaced in Sarah's memory. ". . . I assume you'll want girls who are as obedient and attractive as possible . . ."

Then *were* they to be brides?

The edges of Sarah's heart twisted and shriveled like paper thrown on a bonfire. Maud was in love with Harley. She couldn't be forced to marry some stranger. As for Sarah herself, she didn't intend to marry anyone. She'd made herself that promise years ago after watching Momma suffer daily snubs and unkindness from Papa. No one had the right to force either

her or her cousin to be some stranger's bride. They'd speak to Mr. Dubonnet and explain . . .

He was already on his way back up the narrow staircase. Next moment, he and his sister disappeared onto the deck and the door closed behind them, making it evening once again in the dank compartment.

The smothering claustrophobia swept back, but now being shut in the semi-darkness was only part of Sarah's horror. Worse was the realization of what lay ahead at the end of the voyage. "Maud!" Sarah began, for she needed her cousin to reassure her — to tell her she'd find a way to keep them from having to marry anyone.

Maud had turned away.

"We should uv told 'im we're not big on marrying somebody wot we've never seen before." Lizzie's matter–of–fact voice broke through Sarah's terror. "Though," she added wryly, "if he'd asked polite–like, I wudn't of minded negotiating lunch."

In spite of her panic, Sarah laughed and felt better.

"As for wot 'e said about staying down 'ere," Lizzie nodded toward the stairs, "wot's to stop us openin' that door any time we like an' goin' up into the sunshine?"

"If we do, they might decide to lock it." That thought brought Sarah's claustrophobia rushing back.

"Let 'em. Locks aren't 'ard to pick."

The others must have been as terrified as Sarah for someone started to cry.

Immediately Maud moved forward. "It won't be so bad down here once we get things cleaned up a bit," she said brightly as if her own world hadn't just been shattered into pieces. "First, everyone should choose a bunk."

Immediately four dozen girls hurried to do so.

"We'll take these," Maud told Sarah, taking possession of two middle bunks as she spoke.

The sight of the cramped middle bunks started Sarah shivering again. "I couldn't bear to be sandwiched in between two other people. If we aren't allowed to take a top bunk, I'm going to take a bottom one."

"No, Saree. The floor is too dirty."

"I don't care. I'm taking that one." She pointed to the last bunk in the bottom row nearest the door, directly under one of the tiny portholes.

It seemed Arabella had come to the same conclusion. Even as Sarah spoke, Arabella ran to the end of the row and sat down possessively on the bottom bunk.

Dismayed, Sarah restudied the room. By now all the lower bunks had been taken. So had all the middle ones except for the two Maud was reserving.

Her panic swept back. She had to get out of this sealed room, out into the fresh air —

"'Ere, you take mine an' I'll 'ave the middle one," Lizzie said, clambering out of the bottom bunk directly below the one Maud was saving for Sarah. Her thin face crinkled into a mischievous grin. "But if you start gettin' all panicky an' spoilin' my sleep I'll lean down and swot you one."

"Can I really have your bunk? Don't you mind being in the middle?"

"Wot's to mind?" Lizzie moved her carpet bag to the bunk above. "This might even be warmer. Besides, when you're asleep I kin drop things on you."

Again Sarah giggled and her panic receded.

Lizzie was gazing around. "I think there's blankets," she said, moving toward a shadowy mound behind one of the bulkheads. "There is!" She inspected several, grimaced at the dirt, selected one and took it back to her bunk.

The other girls followed her lead.

After everyone had taken a blanket the pile was still quite high. "Let's git another," Lizzie suggested.

Maud stopped her. "We have to put aside twenty for those older women Mr. Dubonnet said would be traveling with us." She counted out the blankets and put them into a neat pile. Two were left over. "We'll use these for a curtain." Going to the far corner of the compartment where the latrine pails were sitting, she moved them and the chamber pots next to the stairs. Then she hung the two blankets from the rafters above, positioning one so it hid the pails from the sight of anyone going up or down the stairs, and the other so it curtained them from the other people in the compartment. It wasn't exactly privacy, but it was better than no curtain at all.

"We'll have to try to find something to use as covers for those other three pails," Maud began.

No one was listening. At that moment, the door at the top of their stairs opened and a group of women in drab high–necked dresses started down. As they saw the deplorable condition of their new quarters, shocked disbelief registered on their faces.

Five, six, seven Sarah counted. Where were the others? Mr. Dubonnet had said there would be almost three times that number.

At that moment an eighth person appeared at the top of the stairs. To Sarah's surprise, she seemed a lot younger than the others — not much older than Maud. Sarah tried to see her more clearly, but instead of coming right into the compartment, she descended the steps, then moved sideways into the shadows and stood motionless with her face turned away.

The woman who had come down first now stepped forward. Like the others, she was dressed in somber tones, but Sarah couldn't help noticing the stylish cut to her high–necked dress despite its worn spots.

"How do you do," she said in a firm clear voice. "My name is Ruth Rhodes. I, like these other women, am a governess traveling with the assistance of the Female Middle Class Emigration Society. We hope to find work in the colonies." She paused, then added apologetically, "There were to be twenty in our group, but the others have chosen to find space elsewhere on board."

Sarah wondered why these women would leave good jobs in England for the chance of work in the colonies. As each woman in turn was introducing herself, she was trying to think of a polite way to ask. Then the seventh governess provided the answer. She and the others, she explained, no longer had hope of work in England. Their positions had been taken over by graduates of the newly opened Secondary Schools for Women who had skills in science, mathematics and Latin.

The final newcomer was still standing in the shadow of the stairs. "My name is Mary Whitehead," she said in a low, pleasant voice. "I'm a nanny, not a governess. I, too, have been replaced by a high school graduate and am going to the colonies to find work." As she moved to join the others, she continued to stay in the shadows.

Why, Sarah wondered? Then a chance beam of light shone through one of the tiny portholes and for an instant illuminated the young woman's face. A deep red birthmark scarred one cheek. Next moment, the light had gone, and Mary Whitehead's face was once again in shadow.

Each of the governesses in turn picked up a blanket from the pile, selected a top bunk and put her belongings into it.

Lizzie eyed the left-over blankets. Maud had set aside twenty as Mr. Dubonnet had ordered, but only eight had been taken. "'Oo gets them others?" she asked.

No one seemed to know.

Lizzie didn't wait. Crossing the greasy floor, she seized a second blanket, took it back to her bunk and stretched out possessively on top of it.

Ruth Rhodes frowned. "Twelve extra blankets will hardly divide evenly among more than fifty people," she said dryly. "Please put yours back till we agree what should be done with them."

Lizzie pushed the blanket farther behind her. "All the others 'ave a shawl. That's why I need it."

Startled, Sarah poked her head up level with Lizzie's bunk. "I thought you weren't wearing your shawl because you thought they looked so awful."

Lizzie made a face. "They do. But they're better'n freezin'."

"You mean you didn't get one?"

"Matron said I was too disrespectful."

"What did you do?"

"Called 'er Fish. But it weren't on purpose. I didn't know she wos listening."

Sarah burst out laughing, for it hadn't occurred to her before, but Matron did look like a fish.

"If you haven't a shawl," Ruth Rhodes said at last, "then I agree you should be allowed a second blanket to use as one. But I suggest we keep the rest of the extra blankets for people who may be ill."

At the unexpected victory, Lizzie beamed.

"Sarah?" Maud said quietly from the next bunk.

With the arrival of the older women, Sarah

had momentarily forgotten the terrifying truth about where they were going. Now everything rushed back. She turned to her cousin with brimming eyes. "I'm so sorry, Maud. I should never have made you come —"

"Hush, Saree." Maud's voice was soft. "It's going to be all right. When we get to the gold fields, I'll go to whoever is in charge and ask to have word sent back to Harley. Until he can arrange passage home for us, we'll offer to be housemaids."

"They'll never let us."

"Of course they will. After all, it's the church that arranged this trip. They'll listen to Harley." Her voice dropped lower. "But I wanted to speak to you about Lizzie. Try not to make too good a friend of her. I'm afraid she could lead you into trouble."

Maud had been saying the same thing for months, just because Lizzie had been a pick-pocket before she came to the orphanage. As if anyone cared about that. But Sarah knew it would be useless to argue. Instead she said, "What trouble can we get into when we're shut up in this storage compartment?" She was about to add that it didn't matter anyway, considering the fate that waited for them, but Ruth Rhodes was speaking again.

"Now we should decide about those dozen empty top bunks. The fairest thing is to draw lots . . ."

This time no one listened. More than two dozen girls were on their feet and within seconds, all twelve unoccupied top berths had been claimed.

"We probably should have tried for one," Sarah told Lizzie in an undertone.

Lizzie shook her head. "It's better 'ere. We'd never 'ave got two together."

Then bunks and blankets and everything else was forgotten as the ship began to move. Sarah's glance flew to one of the tiny portholes. Through the cobwebs, she could see water moving.

They were underway.

Chapter 7

By mid-afternoon Sarah was seasick — so sea-sick she'd have given everything she possessed to be back at the orphanage, even if it did mean being apprenticed in the mills. By evening she was sorry she'd ever been born.

It was small consolation, but she'd been right about the oil lamps. Watching them sway was fatal.

So was using the latrine pails.

When she wasn't throwing up, she looked with envy at the handful of people who seemed untroubled by the endless rolling motion. Mary and Ruth Rhodes moved from bunk to bunk sponging faces and holding chamber pots as if they'd lived on board all their lives. Surprisingly, Arabella seemed immune to seasickness too, but she made no move to help the others. Instead, she lay in her bunk and slept.

Somewhere Sarah had read that seasickness lasted only three days. Instead of fervently wishing she could die, she tried to remind herself of that. But it didn't help very much as, over and over, the ship rose on its tail like a giant fish, fought to the crest of a forty-foot wave, plunged shivering and shaking down the other side, only to be jerked violently upward again by the even greater wave that followed. She tried to find something stationary to fasten her eyes on, hoping that might stop her head from spinning, but everything moved.

What made things worse was the noise. It wasn't just the continual roar of the steam screw that they seemed to be sitting right on top of, or the howling of the wind, for there was a pattern to both those things. Most unbearable was the unexpected, random crashing of the boxes and barrels in the two cargo bays on either side of them. As the waves tossed the ship about, whatever was stowed there banged into the walls with such force that the sound was a physical blow.

If she was upset by the noise, how much more must her delicate cousin be suffering, Sarah realized, and she tried to call to Maud to make sure she was all right. But it was impossible to make her voice carry over the storm and the crashing of the cargo.

Exhausted, she gave up trying.

The wracking nausea grew steadily worse. Gratefully, she gulped the dippers of cool water that Mary brought several times each day to the suffering girls, and welcomed the momentary relief as her burning face was sponged. But her head throbbed too painfully even to say thank you.

Then, just when Sarah was sure the world would never stop pitching and swaying and reeking of vomit, the seas grew calm. Miraculously, she stopped retching. Pushing back her blanket, she sat up and looked around.

Maud, in the adjoining middle bunk, still lay huddled under her blanket, her face chalk white, her eyes dark with exhaustion.

Frightened, Sarah swung her feet to the floor and moved closer. Maud's hands were icy cold. Pulling her own blanket free, she started tucking it around her cousin.

"'Ere! Don't give 'er that one." Lizzie's dirt-streaked face grinned down from the bunk directly overhead. "You'll need that one yerself."

It was the first time since the journey started that they'd been able to make themselves heard without shouting. The ship still groaned continuously, and the steam screw roared beneath them — but the wind had dropped and there were no more shattering explosions of noise as the sliding cargo struck the end walls of their compartment.

"I'll get yer cousin one of them extras," Lizzie went on, jumping to the floor. Next second she was back holding one of the blankets Ruth Rhodes had said were for sick people.

As Sarah wrapped it around her, Maud opened her eyes and smiled her thanks, then snuggled deeper under the increased warmth.

"I woz 'opin' you'd soon get up," Lizzie told Sarah brightly. "I don't know about you but I'm starvin'." She nodded toward the stairs. "I'm gonna see wot they left us to eat."

Their first afternoon on board, a grinning, curious crewman had left their first week's food supply and a barrel of drinking water at the foot of their stairs. The barrel of water was half empty, for Mary had been parceling it out over the past three days to the seasick girls. But the food sacks were still almost full. Since most of the passengers had been seasick too, and hadn't appeared for meals, Ruth Rhodes had managed to bring back enough from the passengers' table for Mary, Arabella and herself, and for the two or three others who hadn't been bothered by the rolling motion.

Now Lizzie peered into each sack in turn. "Cor!" she said.

The first large sack was filled with uncooked oatmeal. The allowance was printed in large wobbly letters on the outside: Two cups per girl per week. A second large sack held rice. A smaller sack was filled with dried vegetables, and two smaller ones contained tea and raisins.

"That's all we get?" Lizzie protested, staring at the meager rations. "An' wot good is tea an' oatmeal if there's no way to warm them?"

"I'm sure . . . the men in the galley . . . would cook for us . . . if you asked," Maud said in a tight breathless voice from her bunk.

"But we're not allowed to go up on deck, or to talk to anyone," Sarah pointed out. "Besides," she added, glancing toward the stairs and forcing down a rush of smothering fear, "what if that door is locked?" Even voicing the words made her chest tighten.

Lizzie was already scrambling up to see. "It's not locked. It's open!" she called delightedly.

"Surely . . . Mr. Dubonnet . . . won't object . . . to our talking . . . to the cook," Maud continued. "Perhaps Mary would —"

"Oh, no," Mary began in a stricken voice, lifting one hand to her cheek. "I don't think I —"

She had no need to protest further for already Arabella was moving toward the stairs. "*I'll* go speak to him," she said smugly. "I haven't been sick like most of the rest of you." Fluffing out her long wavy hair and smoothing her still clean skirt, she disappeared in the direction of the upper deck.

"Perhaps . . . some of you others," Maud went on in the same breathless voice, "would dump . . . those latrine pails. People could . . . take turns."

Food was forgotten. "Me 'n Sarah'll go first," Lizzie offered. Heading for the corner where Maud had put up the blanket curtain, Lizzie grabbed the nearest pail and started for the stairs. Reaching the top, she opened the door and without even a pause stepped out onto the deck.

For the first time in five days, a narrow path of sunlight shone down into the shadowed compartment. Sarah didn't even stop to consider. Seizing a second pail, she hurried up the stairs after Lizzie. But she hadn't realized what five days of seasickness could do. Rushing up the stairs made her so lightheaded and dizzy she had to lean against the wall to steady herself.

"Wot's wrong? Is dumping them pails goin' to make you sick again?"

"Probably." Sarah waited until her head stopped spinning then continued up the remaining steps. "But staying down there with them undumped would make me sicker." She looked around. Slowly her eyes filled with tears. She'd never known sunshine and fresh air and quiet could be so wonderful.

But Lizzie was staring at a web of heavy ropes that had been strung at waist height all around the deck. "Cor! Look wot them sailors put up so's not to go overboard." Her face crinkled into a grin. "It must 'ave bin as rough up 'ere as wot it were below." For a moment longer she stared, then she carried her pail across the deck to the far rail, lifted it shoulder-high and dumped the contents into the ocean.

It seemed silly to walk way over there, Sarah decided, and she turned to the rail closest to them.

"I 'ope you've lined up somewhere else to sleep tonight, cos yer not sleepin' right under me."

Sarah stopped in confusion. "Pardon?"

"Unless you want to be covered with wot's in that pail, you'd better check where the wind's comin' from."

From the moment they'd come up on deck,

Sarah had been aware of the fresh ocean breeze, but it hadn't occurred to her that it was blowing straight into her face. Grinning self-consciously, she dragged her pail across the deck to the far rail as Lizzie had done.

"Now let's get them other two dumped and go exploring."

"Is that why you were so quick to tell my cousin we'd do the dumping?"

Lizzie smiled impishly. "Gives us an excuse fer bein' up 'ere. I just 'ope not too many others want to share with us." She led the way down for the other two pails.

This time when they came back up, the deck was no longer deserted. Two figures stood by the rail — a crewman, barefoot and shirtless, his pants fastened around his middle with a bit of rope, and a lady of perhaps twenty–seven or eight.

At the sight of the two figures, Lizzie slipped silently out of sight behind one of the lifeboats, but Sarah was too fascinated to do anything but stand and stare.

The lady's dress was of brilliant pink satin with a full skirt and a lower neckline than any Sarah had ever seen before. In fact, she reflected with a grin, one inch lower and nothing would have been left to the imagination at all. The lady's golden hair was framed by a wide-brimmed bonnet of matching pink. Rouge brightened her cheeks and lips. One white-gloved hand held a parasol, and she was looking up at the sailor with laughing eyes.

Who was she? Sarah wondered in delight.

The sailor seemed on the point of saying something when he noticed Sarah. The words went unspoken. He stared.

Sarah felt herself shrivel. In her haste to follow Lizzie out into the fresh air she'd forgotten how she must look — matted hair, streaked face, filthy dress. She'd also forgotten how she must smell!

Mortified, she turned, intending to dump the second pail as quickly as she could and escape back below, but a white-gloved hand joined hers on the handle of the bucket.

"Let me help," said a cheery voice. "From the looks of things, you should be resting up somewhere in the sun, not dumping latrine pails. Were you very sick?"

Sarah was too surprised to be embarrassed. She smiled at the stylish lady and nodded.

Next moment the lady in pink calmly took the pail out of her hand, removed the lid, and without even a grimace of distaste, dumped the contents into the ocean. "Be a good chap, Ned," she told the staring sailor, "and find us some warm water, so Miss — Miss . . ."

"Sarah. Only I've got to go," Sarah supplied quickly, coming out of her daze and accepting the pail back again. "Mr. Dubonnet said we weren't allowed to talk to any of the passengers."

Understanding dawned on the face under the pink bonnet. "Then you're one of the orphanage girls. Has it been dreadful in that cargo compartment?"

Sarah started to say no, but the understanding in the laughing eyes stopped her.
"Yes," she admitted shyly.

The pink lady nodded. "I was supposed to
travel with you, for they'd led us to believe that
the space you were being assigned was roomy
and comfortable. Then Ned told me the truth
about where you were to be quartered." The
hint of a smile sounded in her voice. "I decided
to make other arrangements. But I'm afraid
your Mr. Dubonnet isn't too pleased."

"You mean, you're one of the governess
ladies?"

The smile in the lady's eyes deepened. "Like
them, I'm going to the western colonies to find
work, but I'm not a governess."

Sarah gave a relieved sigh. "I was sure you
couldn't be — Oh!" Her hand flew to her face.
"I didn't mean to be rude. It's just —"

The lady in pink was laughing. "Don't apologize. I'd have been insulted if you'd thought
I was a governess."

Sarah relaxed. "Why did you say Mr. Dubonnet
wouldn't be pleased?"

"Because when I changed my plans some of
the others did too."

"I don't understand."

"It's often difficult for a single woman to travel
alone and not be subject to a certain amount of
unpleasantness," the lady in pink explained.
"Unless she has a maid with her or a traveling
companion, people sometimes judge her unfairly.
So when these governesses decided to set out

on this journey they were quite willing to pay a small extra fee to Mr. Dubonnet if it guaranteed his protection and chaperonage."

"You mean they paid him something in addition to the fare they'd already paid the steamship company?"

The lady in pink nodded.

"So they could live in our compartment!"

At the shocked disbelief in Sarah's tone, the lady again burst out laughing. Then her expression sobered. "Don't be too hard on Mr. Dubonnet. The arrangement suited the governesses as well. Without his offer of chaperonage, many of them might not have risked the long and perhaps dangerous trip. But I'm afraid he may now be in difficulties."

"How do you mean?"

"Struggling student missionaries seldom have much money, and everything on this ship has to be paid for. That includes food, drink, extra services, and any special treats." A frown came into her eyes. "Your Mr. Dubonnet may have been depending on a fee from twenty governesses to finance his journey. Now with only eight hiring his services, he may be forced to find some way to make up the difference."

"But his sister looks as if she has lots of money!"

The lady smiled. "It's his sister's husband who has the money. He may not be willing to share it with Mr. Dubonnet, who doesn't strike me as being too easy to like."

Sarah waited, hoping she would go on. But

at that moment the lady in pink noticed half a dozen ill–kempt crewmen on the other side of the deck who had stopped work to stare at them. Whatever she might have been going to add was forgotten. Casually, she adjusted her position so Sarah was screened from the leering sailors and said quietly, "My name is Bea O'Toole. Next time you come up to dump pails, I'll watch for you."

For the last few minutes, the man she'd called Ned had been so quiet Sarah had almost forgotten he was still there. Now he moved closer. "You wouldn't have to dump pails at all if you'd do what we do." He nodded toward the stern of the ship where a platform had been built hanging low over the water with a grill for a floor. Stretching out onto it were the tail ends of half a dozen ropes. The other ends of the ropes were firmly tied to the railing behind. "It takes practice when the sea's rough, but you're safe enough as long as you don't let go of the ropes."

Sarah couldn't help giggling at the thought of everyone in their compartment coming up here and clutching the end of a rope while they attended to the demands of nature. But next minute she grabbed her empty pail and raced for the stairs, for coming around the deck toward them was Mrs. Worthing.

Sarah didn't think she'd been seen, but she didn't intend to take any chances. She wasn't sure if she was supposed to be up here even to dump the pails, and she certainly wasn't supposed to be up here talking to a sailor.

Eager to tell Lizzie about Bea, she hurried back below. But Lizzie hadn't returned. Sarah was just about to go back up and look for her when Arabella came storming down.

"The cook was horrible! He said he wasn't wasting his time cooking for street girls."

"We're not street girls!" Sarah protested. But even as she spoke she felt herself crumple inside. For the first time she realized that in the eyes of the crew and passengers they *were* street girls. They would also be street girls in the eyes of the miners when they reached the gold fields. They'd be seen as street girls and they would be treated as street girls . . .

"He says we're to take him everything at once for the whole week and he'll cook it all up together. Then we can eat it cold."

In an effort to push away her own frightening thoughts Sarah forced herself to concentrate on what Arabella was saying. "Even our tea and our porridge?"

Arabella nodded. "He said Mrs. Worthing told him cold food would do us fine."

Chapter 8

Sarah had just started back up the stairs in search of Lizzie when she appeared at the top of the sunlit stairway, carrying her pail and grinning.

"Where have you been?" Sarah whispered. She followed Lizzie back down, waited while she dropped her pail behind the curtain and moved to her bunk. "Mrs. Worthing was up there. I was afraid —"

"I know. I saw 'er."

"Did she see you?"

"'Course not. I've found us a place to 'ide." Lizzie's whisper turned bright with excitement. "It's a storage cupboard."

Sarah felt herself shiver. "How could you shut yourself up in a cupboard? What if someone had accidentally locked you in?"

"I left the door open. You don't 'ave to shut it 'cause it's 'alf 'id behind one of them lifeboats." Her face was beaming. "As soon as it's dark tonight, I'll show you."

"We can't go on deck without permission!"

"Nobody'll know if we 'ide in that cupboard." As if that settled the matter, Lizzie said in a different voice, "Wot did that fancy lady 'ave to say?"

Worrying about whether or not they should go on deck was forgotten. "Did you know the governesses had to pay Mr. Dubonnet to travel down here?" In an excited whisper, Sarah repeated everything Bea O'Toole had said.

As she finished, Lizzie let out in a long resigned sigh, "Then I guess we're not so bad off after all."

Sarah stared in surprise. "Pardon?"

Lizzie nodded at the pillowless bunks, the latrine pails, the dark crowded quarters — "Think 'ow we'd 'ate ourselves if we wos payin' out money fer this."

Sarah burst out laughing.

When dinner was over that evening, all the governesses except Mary left the compartment and went up on deck. Mr. Dubonnet couldn't insist they stay below since they'd paid for their passage. The girls watched enviously as the older women disappeared. Then, as it was growing steadily darker in their shadowed compartment and there was nothing else to do, most of them climbed back into their bunks.

"Now?" Lizzie whispered.

Sarah shook her head. "Not till the others are asleep."

Finally, when the last whispering voices had quietened and the darkness was deep enough that Sarah couldn't even see the shape of Lizzie's bunk above her, she agreed to go. But even then she insisted they make it look as if they were just going to use the latrine pails. Grateful for Maud's curtain, she paused a moment behind it, then soundlessly followed Lizzie up the stairs.

"Over 'ere," Lizzie directed, leading the way to a storage locker behind the rack of lifeboats. "See? We kin 'ide in 'ere and not be seen even with the door open. An' there's room for both of us."

Sarah started to crawl in.

"Not now! Only if we 'ave to. Let's 'ave a look round."

Sarah shrank back into the shadows, for clusters of people were sauntering on deck enjoying the warm summer evening. "They'll see us and tell Mr. Dubonnet."

"Not if we look like we belong." Lifting her chin, Lizzie moved with calm self–assurance out of the shadows.

"Come back!" Sarah whispered, but Lizzie was halfway across the open deck. The spot she was headed for was on the far rail, a little removed from any of the groups of passengers and not in the direct glow of the ship's oil lamps. Still Sarah expected at any moment that someone would point at her and shout that she was supposed to be below.

No one paid any attention.

Reaching the rail, Lizzie settled herself comfortably and stared out at the tumbling ocean waves as if she had nothing else to do. Then, straightening the blanket she was using as a shawl, she sauntered leisurely back and rejoined Sarah. Her face was beaming. "Now it's your turn. Dare you."

Sarah stared at her in horror. For sure she'd be caught. She knew she would. But a person couldn't refuse a Dare. Trying to look as calm and self-assured as Lizzie had looked, she stepped tentatively out of the shadows.

Someone was moving toward her . . .

Abandoning all attempts to look self-confident, Sarah ran. On reaching the rail, she stopped in the darkest spot. She'd stay just long enough to fulfill Lizzie's Dare, she told herself, then escape back to their compartment. And next time Lizzie suggested something like this she'd —

A hand closed over her arm. "What are you doing up here?"

Sarah's heart stopped beating. Slowly, she turned around, frantically trying to think of an excuse Mrs. Worthing would accept. But it wasn't Mrs. Worthing. It was Bea O'Toole smiling down at her.

Sarah clutched the rail while she tried to stop shaking.

"I gather you're not supposed to be up here," Bea said, her eyes twinkling. "Don't worry, I won't give you away. But if you're planning to come up often, we've got to do something about that gingham uniform." She frowned thoughtfully for a minute. "Perhaps one of those small flowered tablecloths from the passenger dining room would do to cover your skirt. I'll ask Ned to see if he can find a spare one." The twinkle in her eyes deepened. "Two spare ones, so that friend of yours can have one too."

"Did you see . . ."

Bea nodded, but a male passenger was coming toward them. "Meet me here tomorrow evening," she said quickly, and moved away.

Hurrying back to join Lizzie, Sarah repeated what Bea had said.

Next evening as promised, Bea was waiting with two flowered tablecloths. They hid the skirts of the gingham uniforms perfectly, and Sarah's shawl and Lizzie's extra blanket covered the tops.

"As soon as it's dark, let's circle the ship with them tablecloths on," Lizzie whispered excitedly.

Sarah shook her head. She'd resolved last night to stay out of Lizzie's schemes from now on.

"You mean not tonight or not never?"

"Not ever!"

Instead of looking downcast, Lizzie merely grinned, for a person couldn't refuse a Dare. If some night she repeated her challenge, they both knew Sarah would have to accept.

Chapter 9

With the end of the seasickness, Mr. Dubonnet and Mrs. Worthing began taking turns chaperoning a daily exercise walk for the girls. Promptly at eleven each morning, all those who were well enough were met at the top of their staircase and marched two by two in caterpillar procession around the deck for forty-five minutes.

"Why don't you come with us?" Sarah asked Mary one morning, noticing that the rest of the governesses spent most of each day on deck, but Mary only went up after dark.

"Sometime, perhaps," Mary replied. Then she smiled wryly. "It's not much fun meeting strangers."

Sarah's heart twisted. "Because they stare? But you don't mind us looking at you?"

"You're used to me. That's the way it always works. At the last place where I was a nanny the children stared at me open-mouthed for the first few days, and my mistress tried to avoid looking at me at all. Then everyone got used to me and didn't even notice this any more." Her hand brushed her cheek. She smiled. "As soon as other people forget about it, I do too."

Sarah didn't say any more about Mary coming with them, for she knew Mary would certainly be stared at. All the girls were stared at. That was why Sarah hated these walks so much. From the moment they had appeared on deck the very first time everyone on board knew who they were and where they were going. Now crowds of passengers and crewmen gathered each day to watch them. Some had even begun positioning themselves outside the girls' quarters a few minutes before eleven in the morning. When the girls appeared, the men moved closer, forcing the young orphans to brush against them to get through. Then for the whole forty–five minute walk they followed, making jokes and smirking. Arabella thought it was fun, but it made Sarah feel sick inside.

One morning she pretended to be ill so she wouldn't have to go. She wished her cousin would stay below, too, for Maud was coughing more and more, and walking for that length of time seemed to exhaust her. But Maud merely smiled and insisted she was fine.

However, when the walk was over, Maud was visibly shaken. It seemed several of the men had singled her out and been particularly brash and insulting.

It wasn't just the staring that made Sarah feel sick inside — it was the daily reminder of what lay ahead at the end of the voyage. In the privacy of her lower bunk, she took Penelope out of her carpetbag. "To help in the dark places," Momma had said. Maybe the other girls would think going–on–sixteen was too grown up for rag dolls, but that didn't seem so important any longer.

"Things will get easier," Maud's soft voice sounded beside her.

Embarrassed, Sarah pushed Penelope out of sight.

Next day when it was time for their walk, Sarah planned to play sick again, but her absence the previous morning must have been noticed. Mary's, too, for at a few minutes before eleven, Mrs. Worthing arrived in their quarters with orders that everyone was to accompany her up on deck. "And you, Mary, must come too," she said to the young nanny. "Mr. Dubonnet has noticed that you stay below all the time. He says it's not healthy, and you are to come up with the other girls."

Sarah glanced quickly across the compartment. If it was awful for her when the men stared and made crude jokes, how much more awful would it be for Mary? She moved beside her as they went up on deck. "If we stay in the middle, we won't be noticed so much," she whispered.

Mary nodded gratefully.

The plan worked. If any of the staring men noticed Mary's birthmark, they didn't say anything.

When the walk was almost over Sarah suggested moving up in line past the other girls so they'd be the first to go back below. She led the way, and was just within sight of their stairway when she glimpsed someone running up from the compartment and hurrying away.

She told the others, but they didn't believe her. Even Mary had seen no one. Everyone insisted she must have imagined the intruder, because she hated so much being stared at. She didn't argue for she had no proof. She couldn't even make a guess as to who it had been, for she'd only seen the man's back. But she knew she hadn't imagined it.

She wondered what he'd been doing in their quarters, and if he'd sneak down again some other morning when they were all out walking. For more than a week she tried to watch while they were on deck, but if he came back, he took care to be in and out of their compartment before the walk was over.

Chapter 10

By now, Sarah was more worried about her cousin than she wanted to admit, for Maud's cough seemed to be growing worse instead of better. Sarah also suspected she might be running a fever. One minute her hands would be icy cold, and the next wet with perspiration. She begged Maud to speak to Mrs. Worthing and ask for help, but Maud simply smiled and said she was no sicker than lots of the others and that she'd be fine in another few days.

But she was sicker than any of the others. Much sicker. Sometimes at night when it was damp and cold she seemed hardly able to get her breath. Sarah grew more and more frightened.

The only thing that helped was escaping for a little while in the evenings with Lizzie, after the rest of the girls in the compartment were asleep. They never stayed long on deck — just half an hour — but the fresh air and the moonlight and the peaceful silence helped for a little while to drive away the fear and the terror.

One night, she and Lizzie made their usual stealthy exit using the curtain in front of the latrine pails as a shield. When they emerged onto the deck they discovered a sky-blue shawl hanging forgotten on the back of a chair.

"Finders keepers!" Lizzie cried, darting over and picking it up.

"It isn't finders keepers, it's stealing," Sarah told her acidly. "As soon as the owner remembers where she left it, she'll be back."

A thoughtful expression crossed Lizzie's face. "Then I won't snitch it," she said after a moment. "But I'll try it on." Before Sarah could protest, she dropped the blanket from her shoulders and wrapped the sky-blue shawl around herself instead. Then she moved to the window of one of the inside deck cabins. "Cor," she breathed in wonder, gazing at her reflection in the glass. "Don't I look special?"

Sarah had to admit she did, for the blue of the fancy shawl set off Lizzie's light hair and green eyes perfectly. But at any moment the owner might come back. "Lizzie, take it off!"

Reluctantly, Lizzie obeyed. She took the shawl from around her shoulders, held it against her cheek for a moment, then placed it gently back on the chair where she'd found it. "Wudn't it be somethin' to 'ave a shawl like that?" she said softly. She put her drab blanket back on.

"Would you really have stolen that shawl and kept it if I hadn't said anything?"

"'Course I wud."

Sarah was so surprised at Lizzie telling the truth that it must have shown on her face.

For the first time Lizzie's smile faltered. "You thought I'd lie." Disbelief and hurt edged her voice. "You're my friend. Didn't you know I'd always tell you the truth?" She turned away.

"Lizzie, wait!" Sarah cried. She wanted to explain, for she'd seen the pain in Lizzie's eyes.

If Lizzie heard she gave no sign. Already she was almost out of sight.

Sarah started after her.

One of the other girls must have been sleepless and come up on deck too, for another gingham uniform was disappearing down the stairs ahead of Lizzie. Who was it? Sarah wondered, hoping she wouldn't report them to Mrs. Worthing. But there was no time now to find out, for Lizzie was already part way down the stairs. In another minute she'd be swallowed up by the shadows. "Lizzie!" Sarah called again.

Then, as she reached the bottom, she stopped in relief, for a uniformed figure was standing waiting in the semi–darkness.

"Lizzie, please let me explain. I —"

It wasn't Lizzie after all, but Arabella. That must be who had gone down the stairs a few minutes ago, Sarah realized with a shock. Would Arabella report them? More important, had Arabella seen Lizzie put on that shawl? If so, did she think Lizzie had been planning to steal it? Sarah knew she should stop and explain, but first she had to straighten things out with Lizzie. That was more important. Besides, Arabella might not have seen Lizzie with the shawl, in which case a long explanation would do more harm than good. Better to wait, she decided, and brushing past Arabella without speaking, she hurried across the compartment.

Lizzie was lying with her face turned to the wall.

"Lizzie?" Sarah whispered. "Lizzie?"

Lizzie didn't answer.

Next morning, to Sarah's relief, the incident seemed to have been forgotten. Then something happened that put the blue shawl out of both their minds.

Each Friday morning since the voyage had started the girls' weekly supply of food was delivered to their compartment by one of the crewmen. Each week the amounts were exactly the same.

Until today. This time the supply of oatmeal, rice, dried vegetables and tea would divide up into only six daily portions instead of seven.

"We must have filled the measure too full," Maud said, remembering the chef's words on the first day when he'd given them a large tin measuring cup together with their first week's rations. The cup had a line marked on it, and the chef had made it clear that was the line they were to use. "Next week we'll be more careful," Maud said, taking back enough from each of the six portions to make a seventh.

The following week they took extra care to fill the measure exactly right, but still the oatmeal, rice and dried vegetables would stretch to only six of their usual portions. As for the tea and raisins, there seemed to be hardly more than half the usual amounts of them.

"The tea and raisins is the best part!" Lizzie complained, "Even if the tea is cold."

It was true. The girls looked forward all day to the small handful of raisins and the tea that they had with supper.

"We'll look forward to — tea and raisins — every other night," Maud said in breathy bunches, making it sound as if that would be no particular hardship. But as soon as the supplies were divided and carefully put away, she wrapped her shawl tightly around her shoulders and, ignoring Mrs. Worthing's orders, left the compartment and went up to the galley.

At first the cook refused to listen. Then he admitted reluctantly that some of the crewmen or passengers might be tempted to help themselves to extra tea and raisins and even oatmeal if they saw them lying around unattended — for provisions on board the *Tynemouth* were strictly rationed for everyone. But he didn't offer to do anything about it.

"I'll speak to Mr. Dubonnet," Maud told the others.

On their walk next morning she did so. He seemed shocked, but could make no suggestions as to which of the crew members or passengers might be responsible.

Then, several evenings later, Fanny was discovered in tears. The little brooch that her mother had given her had disappeared. "It w–w–were the only special thing me mum ever owned," she explained quietly. "When she was sent to the w–w–workhouse, she gave it to me. I brought it with me wrapped up in there." She pointed to her carpetbag.

Immediately, Arabella looked accusingly at Lizzie.

To Sarah's dismay, so did several of the others. They must be just following Arabella's lead, she told herself, for they couldn't know about the blue shawl. Though some of them could have seen Lizzie checking out that carpetbag the morning they were leaving. Certainly Arabella had . . .

The silence continued to stretch out. "Perhaps your brooch has fallen into a corner, or under your bunk," Sarah said in an attempt to change the direction of everyone's thoughts.

Fanny turned her carpetbag inside out while the other girls searched the floor, but there was no sign of the brooch.

The following week, Maud's leather-bound book of poems disappeared.

Every afternoon since the voyage had started, Maud had taken it out of her carpetbag and silently read and reread Harley's poems — particularly the one he'd read to her the morning they were leaving — *"You'll not be with me when the spring is here . . ."* Each afternoon as she'd read, some of her illness seemed to drop away.

But today when she'd gone as usual to get Harley's book, it wasn't there.

"Maybe it slipped out onto the blanket."

"Did you leave it in somebody else's bunk?"

"Look on the floor."

Suggestions flew, but the book was nowhere to be found.

"I know 'ow bad I'd feel if I could read an' that book 'ad been mine," Lizzie said. "One of them crewmen wot hang around the stairs must 'ave snitched it."

Arabella glanced over in disgust. "Why would one of them take it when most of them probably can't read?"

"Maybe one of 'em took it so's 'e could sell it." Lizzie turned to Sarah. "You saw one of 'em coming up from our quarters one day. Remember? Maybe 'e came again today. Maybe when we wos all up on deck 'e crept down, snitched your cousin's book, an' left again."

"Or maybe you did," Arabella said spacing the words so they hung on the air. "You left the walk in the middle this morning and came back. I know because I saw you."

Every pair of eyes turned and stared at Lizzie.

"To use them latrine pails," Lizzie retorted, her green eyes blazing. "'Cos I 'ad to. Mrs. Worthing said I could."

Arabella rubbed her chin thoughtfully. "I'm trying to remember," she said innocently. "Did you go below to use the latrine pails the morning Fanny's brooch disappeared?"

Lizzie's face flushed scarlet. "I'm no thief! I didn't touch that brooch, nor Maud's book!"

But as Arabella continued to smirk, Sarah could feel the suspicion building in the dingy compartment.

"They don't really believe you took any of those things," she tried to tell Lizzie later that evening. "By tomorrow they'll realize that Arabella is just making trouble."

But instead of subsiding, the suspicion grew, for when Sarah and Lizzie went up on deck to dump the latrine pails, Arabella told the others about the blue shawl.

"You should have spoken up and defended Lizzie," Sarah snapped when her cousin told her what had happened. "You know Arabella doesn't like Lizzie. She's just trying to make trouble!"

"But she says she saw Lizzie put on the shawl, and that right now she probably has it hidden away in her carpetbag."

"She put it on just to see how she looked. She took it right off again, and Arabella knows that. If she saw Lizzie put it on she must have seen her take it off." But even as she spoke Sarah realized that might not be true, for Lizzie had no longer been standing in full view on the open deck. She'd moved away to look at her reflection in that cabin window.

"I never took nothin'," Lizzie whispered to Sarah for the dozenth time. "You know I didn't. I never took that brooch, nor your cousin's book, nor any extra rations." For the girls were beginning to whisper that Lizzie must have stolen those too. "It 'as to 'ave been one of them crewmen."

"Then tell the others that," Sarah urged. "They won't listen to me. You've got to talk to them yourself."

Lizzie tossed her head and put on her brightest smile. "Wot do I care wot they think?"

By now the others had remembered that Lizzie had been a pickpocket before coming to the orphanage, and were deliberately avoiding her. She started spending more and more time alone on deck, hiding long hours in the storage cupboard.

"Tell them you didn't take anything," Sarah urged.

"'Oo cares wot they think?" Lizzie repeated.

Chapter 11

Lizzie no longer asked Sarah to go with her up on deck in the evenings. Instead she went alone. "If anybody sees you slippin' out with me, they'll turn on you too," she said, "an' wot's the use of that?" But they still went together in the mornings when it was their turn on pail duty.

One morning as they came up on deck, Ruth Rhodes was standing by the rail talking to Mrs. Worthing.

"Cor!" Lizzie breathed, pointing at Mrs. Worthing's brown leather boots. They were mid-calf height with a row of tiny buttons up the front. She looked from them to her own black orphanage boots and for the first time in days, the twinkle came back into her eyes. "D'you think she might consider a trade?"

Sarah burst out laughing.

". . . permission to use the fireplace in your cabin to heat water for our tea?" Ruth Rhodes was saying. "One of the girls in particular is quite ill. If she could have hot tea —"

"Oh, dear, no." Mrs. Worthing's voice carried clearly. "If there is illness below, I couldn't take a chance on having it carried upstairs for fear Mr. Dubonnet might catch it. He often comes up to my stateroom in the evenings, bringing a little tea and oatmeal, and fixes something extra to eat." She smiled. "What would happen to all of us if Mr. Dubonnet were to fall ill?" Her voice dropped to a confidential whisper. "The church leaders in Victoria would never forgive any of us." She simpered. "It isn't official yet, but I think they are planning to offer him an important position of some kind."

Lizzie waited till Mrs. Worthing and Ruth Rhodes had moved half a dozen paces away then said quietly, "I'm goin' to see."

"Pardon?"

"If she really 'as a fireplace in 'er room." Dumping the contents of her pail over the side, Lizzie ran along the deck.

Sarah knew she should call her back, but it was days since she'd seen Lizzie so excited and cheerful. Besides, it should be safe enough. No one was in sight but Mrs. Worthing and Miss Rhodes, and they were walking the other way. Dumping her own pail, Sarah hurried after Lizzie.

Mrs. Worthing's stateroom was in the bow of the ship next to the captain's cabin, and according to Bea O'Toole was the most luxurious on board. Bea said the steamship owner was a friend of Mrs. Worthing's husband and had arranged for her to use the fancy cabin on the voyage.

Two large portholes looked out onto the deck. Lizzie was peering in through one of them. "There *is* a fireplace! With an 'ook for a kettle! An' look at them clothes!" Her pointing finger thumped against the glass. "A pink dress an' a yellow one, an' a second pair of fancy boots!"

For a moment Sarah stood peering through the other porthole, then she took a firm hold of Lizzie's arm and pulled her away. She knew at any second Mrs. Worthing and Ruth Rhodes would reach the end of the deck and turn back.

"We've got to try on them clothes," Lizzie protested.

"No."

"Not right now in the daylight, but tonight." Lizzie's eyes were dancing. "It's time we started going up on deck again. We kin —"

"No! If we were caught in Mrs. Worthing's cabin . . ."

"We wudn't be."

"How can you be sure? Even if you make it a Dare we're still not going to do it," Sarah said firmly.

Lizzie breathed a resigned sigh. "I s'pose you're right. But I wish you weren't." Her voice grew wistful. "All me life I've wondered wot I'd look like if I'd been born a fine lady."

Chapter 12

Lizzie said nothing more about the dresses in Mrs. Worthing's closet, and Sarah hoped she'd forgotten about them. Then several nights later, something happened that gave both their thoughts a new direction.

As usual, Lizzie had slipped up on deck by herself and hidden in the storage cupboard rather than spend the evening facing the cold, unfriendly glances of the other girls. She stayed longer than usual, and Sarah was starting to worry when Lizzie reappeared on the stairs.

"Why have you been so long?" Sarah asked in a worried whisper as Lizzie crawled into her bunk.

Lizzie swung her head over the side. Her eyes were shining with excitement. "I think I've found out 'oo's bin taking our food, an' 'oo snitched the brooch and that book."

"Who?"

"Shhh!" Lizzie cautioned. Her eyes were twinkling. "I don't want to say till I'm sure. But tomorrow night I'm going to 'ave a little talk to 'im, face to face."

"Talk with who?"

"The person wot snitched our things."

"I'll come with you. It's too dangerous to go alone."

"'Ow could it be dangerous?" Lizzie said in disgust.

Next evening as Lizzie was preparing to start up the stairs, Sarah again suggested they should go together.

"Two of us might scare 'im away," Lizzie replied. "But I'll tell you all about it soon as I get back." She disappeared.

Sarah waited impatiently. It seemed forever before she heard soft footsteps coming back down the shadowed stairs. She waited till Lizzie crawled into the space overhead, then sat up and peeked over the boards of the bunk. "So tell me!" she whispered excitedly.

Lizzie had turned her face to the wall.

"Tell me what happened."

Still no answer.

Getting out of her own bunk, Sarah leaned into Lizzie's. "Please tell me what's wrong."

Slowly Lizzie turned back. Her face was white and frightened. "All I wanted wos for 'im to admit he took them things so I could explain to the others." Her voice was so low Sarah had to strain to hear. "So's they'd stop thinking I

snitched things. I wudn't 'ave made trouble for
'im. Only 'e wudn't believed me. 'E said I would
make trouble so 'e'd 'ave to fix it so I couldn't."

"What did he mean, fix it?" Sarah asked
sharply. "What did he say he'd do?"

For a long moment, Lizzie plaited the edge of
her rough grey blanket with hands that weren't
steady. At last, talking more to herself than to
Sarah, she said, "I wudn't 'ave made trouble.
Why wudn't 'e believe me?"

"Who was it, Lizzie? Tell me! Who did you go
to meet?"

Lizzie looked up. For a moment Sarah
thought she was going to answer. Then she
shook her head. "If I tell you, 'e'll 'ave it in for
you too."

"I don't care! Tell me!"

But Lizzie shook her head once more.
Turning in her bunk she again faced the wall.

Chapter 13

All the next day Sarah tried to make Lizzie talk about what had happened, but Lizzie stuck to what she'd said before, that it would just get Sarah in trouble too.

When it came time for the morning walk, Lizzie pretended to be sick and stayed behind. She did the same thing again the next morning, and the next, not even going up to help Sarah when it was their day to dump pails. But by the time four days had passed and nothing awful had happened, she began to feel better.

Sarah was relieved, for she had enough to worry about with Maud. They'd been at sea six weeks now, and Maud continued to grow sicker. For more than a week she had been too ill to go up on deck at all, and for the past few days had stayed in her bunk even for meals.

"I'm so sorry I dragged you along on this awful journey," Sarah told her one night between bouts of Maud's coughing. She was sitting beside her cousin's bunk. "We should never have come."

For a moment the familiar twinkle appeared in Maud's tired eyes. "And right this minute . . . you could be having a wonderful time . . . working in the mills."

In spite of herself, Sarah smiled. "It couldn't be worse than this."

"Yes, it could. This will end, Saree . . . and knowing that . . . makes it bearable."

"But then what's going to be in store for us?" Sarah's voice was low and frightened. She bit her lip to stop it trembling. For the past little while with so much happening, she'd almost forgotten what waited for them at the end of the journey. Now everything rushed back.

Maud's hand closed over hers. "They won't force us to be brides when they hear about Harley," she said softly. For a moment another bout of coughing interrupted, then she went on, "They'll let us be maids or nannies, or take some other job." Her face relaxed in a smile. "I'm glad we came, Saree. I've a feeling the chance . . . is going to come . . . for the exciting adventure you've dreamed about . . . and when it does, you must take it."

For the first time, Sarah found herself thinking of the end of the voyage with a glimmer of hope instead of terror.

That evening she was happier than she'd

been since the trip started.

Except for her worry about her cousin. That was increasing, because the weather was starting to get colder.

It was almost two weeks now since they'd left the warm waters near the equator and started pushing farther and farther into the southern hemisphere. Now, when the girls went up on deck, they wore both cotton shifts one on top of the other underneath their gingham uniforms, their shawls over top, and sometimes their bed blankets wrapped around them as well. Even so, the biting wind chilled them through. By the time the ship reached the tip of Cape Horn there might even be snow, for Cape Horn was as far south of the equator as Greenland was north.

As the weather grew colder, Maud's coughing grew worse.

Two mornings later when Sarah was dumping pails, she told Bea about her cousin. "Each day she seems to get sicker. Maybe it's because our compartment is so cold."

Bea's glance narrowed. "Has she a bad cough?"

"Sometimes she can hardly get her breath. And I think she has a fever too. Lots of nights she sleeps hardly at all."

"What does Mrs. Worthing say about it?"

"I don't think she knows." Keeping her voice carefully neutral, Sarah added, "I think both Mrs. Worthing and Mr. Dubonnet avoid coming down to our compartment in case of infection."

The lines around Bea's mouth tightened.

"When they seem to dislike us so much," Sarah went on in a low, puzzled tone, "why did they offer to chaperone us on this voyage?"

"Because being accepted into the ranks of the clergy is almost the only way a man of mediocre parentage and education can climb up the social ladder." An acid note had crept into Bea's voice. "Clergy are universally respected and admired. Dubonnet is hoping his strict supervision of you girls will please his church employers enough that they will admit him into their ranks."

Sarah had a sudden memory of Uncle Tor with his gentle kindness and understanding — Uncle Tor who had died because he had insisted on taking communion to the sick in his parish who were ill with smallpox. Tears sprang up hot behind her eyelids. What would Uncle Tor think of a man like Mr. Dubonnet being made a —

"Don't worry about your cousin," Bea's words broke through Sarah's distress. "I'll see if I can find something that will help her."

Next morning Bea was waiting with two small boxes in her hands. "Cough powders for your cousin and anyone else who needs them, and laudanum for Maud to help her sleep. Give her two or three drops, or even more, if she needs it." She handed Sarah the boxes.

"Where did you get them?" Sarah said gratefully.

The twinkle was back in Bea's eyes. "From

the ship's doctor. But if he hadn't had anything I'd have tried the ship's black market."

Sarah's confusion must have shown.

"Poor Captain McLaughlin does his best to make sure everyone is well looked after," Bea went on, "but the ship's owner is more interested in making a profit. He charges for everything including medical supplies. As a result, if people have anything to spare, they buy and sell among themselves."

"How much did you have to —"

"Nothing," Bea replied, her tone innocent but her eyes laughing. "When you can't buy or sell, it's often possible to barter." She moved away.

Sarah took the medicine below.

"I don't mind lying awake," Maud said, refusing the laudanum. Her voice was hardly strong enough to be heard over the roar of the steam screw. "It gives me time to think. But I'll try the cough powders."

They didn't seem to help.

By now Sarah was really frightened. More and more often she took Penelope out from under her blanket and held her tightly.

One morning when she was dumping pails she told Bea about Penelope.

"I'd like to have known your mother," Bea said softly when Sarah had finished. "She was right, you know. Life has lots of dark places." She wrapped her wool cloak more tightly around her. "I wonder how different things might have been if someone had cared enough to make a Penelope for me." She moved away.

Then one morning the following week Bea was waiting with an excited smile. "Tell your cousin to hang on for just a few more days. Ned tells me the captain is planning to put in at the Falkland Islands for reprovisioning."

"The Falkland Islands?"

"Near the tip of South America. We reach them just before we round the Cape. Ned says we'll anchor in Stanley Harbor for almost a week. Mind you, it's not going to be all that warm, for I hear there's snow there, but it will be better than being cooped up below decks. And you should be able to get all the fresh fruit and milk you want."

Sarah could hardly wait to get below to tell the others. For the first time in weeks the dreary compartment rang with excited chatter.

"First thing I'm gonna do when we get there is eat two dozen oranges one after the other," one girl whispered.

"I'm 'aving a hot bath and staying in it all night."

"I want to f–f–feel the sun on me cheeks," Fanny said.

"What do you want to do when we get there, Maud?" Sarah asked.

"See the searchlight," Maud answered softly. "I've . . . read about it. It's at Cape Pembroke . . . down the coast from . . . Stanley Harbor." She glanced toward one of the cobwebbed portholes as if the light were already visible. "Night and day it . . . sweeps in a steady circle. They say . . . it has saved more lives than any other searchlight in the world." It was more than she'd managed to say for days and the effort had exhausted her, but as she lay back and closed her eyes she was smiling.

Sarah had a sudden picture of a bright light high up on a cliff side, striking out into the darkness, leading some foundering ship through crashing waves to safety.

The others must have been thinking the same thing for the room fell silent.

Chapter 14

"As you probably know," Mrs. Worthing announced next morning as the crocodile line was forming on deck, "we will be docking shortly at Stanley Harbor in the Falkland Islands for reprovisioning." She smoothed down her skirt with nervous hands. "The regular passengers, of course, will go ashore, but Mr. Dubonnet has decided it will be safer for you girls to stay on board."

Shocked silence greeted her words.

For a moment, Sarah was too stunned to think clearly. How could she break that news to her cousin when she went back below? They'd both been counting on those days on dry land to start Maud feeling better.

"It's for your own safety," Mrs. Worthing defended. "Mr. Dubonnet is experienced in such matters, and knows the dangers you might be subject to if you were to go ashore."

"How typical of that man," Bea told Sarah with disgust next morning as the news of Mr. Dubonnet's ruling spread over the ship. "Tell your cousin I'll bring back some fresh fruit and milk for her." In a deceptively innocent tone she added, "Also, keep in mind that staying on board doesn't mean staying in your quarters. There will be no one here to enforce that rule. Except for a skeleton crew to look after the safety of the ship, everyone else will be ashore."

Sarah hurried below to tell Maud and the others what Bea had said.

The following day the *Tynemouth* docked in Stanley Harbor. Seven of the eight governesses in the below decks compartment put on their cloaks and went up on deck. Only Mary remained below with the girls. Sarah didn't need to ask why. *It's not much fun meeting strangers*, Mary had said.

The girls watched through the cobwebbed portholes as the passengers went ashore. They watched as all but a handful of the crew followed. They watched as the skeleton crew that had been left behind moved the ship back from the dock and dropped anchor in the center of the large, landlocked harbor. Then hesitantly, a few of them went up the stairs and onto the deck.

No one took any notice. The few remaining sailors were busy with their duties and didn't even glance in the girls' direction.

Several more of the girls ventured up into the fresh air, and when there was still no reaction, the others followed. Sarah, Mary and Maud were the last, for Maud needed help climbing the stairs. But once up on deck, they settled her in a sheltered spot in the sunshine and she seemed to feel better.

"Hot tea will make you feel better still," Mary told her cheerily and disappeared in the direction of the galley. Ten minutes later she was back, not only with hot tea but with the news that the few sailors still on board had agreed the girls could use the galley whenever they wanted to heat their porridge, rice and vegetables.

Sarah had forgotten how wonderful hot food could taste. She'd forgotten, too, what it was like to be able to spend more time in the fresh air and sunshine. Admittedly the weather was cold, but with bed blankets converted to temporary cloaks, it was possible to stay on deck for at least an hour or two during the warmest part of each day. Magically, everyone started to feel better.

Everyone except Maud. Despite Sarah and Mary bundling her up and taking her into the fresh air whenever it was warm enough, Maud grew steadily weaker. Each day the others seemed to move about more and more energetically, but Maud was now too ill to walk any distance at all.

One afternoon, Sarah brought Penelope up on deck, hidden in the folds of her shawl. Shyly, she held the doll out to her cousin.

Maud's eyes lit with pleasure. She took the doll as if she were some fragile treasure. "For the dark places. Isn't that what your momma said when she gave Penelope to you?"

Sarah nodded. "And to listen to dreams."

A soft smile lit Maud's face. "Don't ever stop telling her your dreams, Saree." Her hands cradled the doll. "We were right to come — no matter what happens."

Sarah didn't take Penelope back at bedtime.

Each evening, Sarah counted off the days in port until the passengers would be back and Bea would bring the fresh fruit and milk she had promised for Maud. "Only today and tomorrow," she told Mary in a quiet whisper on their fifth morning in Port Stanley Harbor. They were sitting beside Maud who had dozed off.

Mary nodded. "I know how hard it must be for you just waiting." Her low voice was hard to hear over the sound of Maud's labored breathing. "I have a sister, too."

Sarah looked up in surprise. It was the first time Mary had said anything about her family.

"She's just a child still — only twelve — but I miss her. I've promised that as soon as I get a position with a good family out in the colonies and can save the money, I'll bring her out to live with me."

That evening the weather changed. The wind picked up and the temperature dropped. Even in Port Stanley's inland harbor the water started turning over in huge rolling waves.

The next day was worse.

"There's a bad storm down the coast," one of the few remaining sailors on board explained. "No way Cap'n will call the passengers back now till it passes, for he won't risk starting out."

"But he said five or six days," Sarah protested. "Already it's been seven."

"If necessary he'll wait a fortnight."

It was impossible for anyone to stay more than a few minutes on deck now, for the wind was biting and the ship rocked violently. Once again the girls found themselves spending most of each day in their crowded compartment.

The stationary ship grew colder and colder. It was hard to stop shivering long enough to fall asleep. And the ceaseless moaning of the wind, no longer muffled by the movement of the ship, wore on everyone's nerves.

By now Maud was eating hardly anything. The warm tea was all Sarah could convince her to swallow. "You'll feel better when Bea gets back with the fresh fruit and milk," Sarah told her over and over, convincing herself it was true.

On the twelfth day the wind began to drop. That evening, for the first time in almost a week, it was warm enough to go up on deck. With Mary's help, Sarah bundled Maud in blankets and half-lifted her up the stairs. Finding a sheltered corner under the night sky, they settled Maud comfortably. While Mary went below to make some hot tea, Sarah sat down beside her cousin and watched the harbor searchlight push back the darkness.

"Could you prop me up . . . a bit higher?" Maud asked after a few moments. "So I can see the . . . searchlight better." The words were interrupted for breath.

Sarah had brought their bed blankets up on deck. Now she made a mound of them and propped it behind Maud's shoulders.

"I'd like to think when we die . . . we're like that light," Maud went on, watching the moving arc. "Shining down, keeping watch on what's happening . . . maybe sometimes . . . brightening the darkness for someone."

"Maud, don't talk like that. You're going to be fine . . ."

"I'm not scared, Saree." Maud turned to look at her, and for a moment the familiar calmness and assurance shone in her face. "I thought dying would be scary — but it isn't."

Sarah wanted to tell her again not to be silly — that she was going to be fine, but a lump had come into the back of her throat and she couldn't form the words.

For a few minutes there was silence, then Maud said softly, "I wish I still had Harley's poems so you could read them to me." In a soft, faraway voice she recited:

*"You won't be with me though the spring is here.
But I'll remember other happier springs
When distance did not part us."*

Her soft voice faded out.

Sarah took Maud's hand and held it tight as

she blinked away her tears, for she knew the words had been spoken to Harley, not to her.

The talking had exhausted Maud. She leaned back against the blankets. But just as Sarah was sure she was drifting off to sleep, Maud's eyes opened. "If you're going adventuring, Saree, you'll need this." She held out Penelope.

For a moment her hoarse breathing was the only sound, then her soft voice started again. "Saree, make sure you know . . . what you're really looking for . . . on your adventure. And once you do . . . don't let anything . . . stand in your way. Promise?"

It was impossible to speak. All Sarah could do was nod.

That seemed enough. Maud closed her eyes, and this time did drift off to sleep. When Mary returned with the tea, neither she nor Sarah had the heart to waken her.

For a long time the only sound was the water plopping against the hull of the ship, and the subdued hushing of the wind.

Gradually it grew colder. Sarah knew she should take her cousin back below, but she looked so peaceful she hated to disturb her. She was lying with her eyes closed, her face turned toward the searchlight, and she seemed to be smiling.

"We'd better go back inside now," Sarah said at last.

There was no answer.

It was a long moment before she understood why.

Next day, when the crew and passengers came back, they buried Maud in the Port Stanley cemetery in the circular path of the searchlight. Through her tears Sarah wondered if Maud knew. She hoped so. She knew Maud would like that.

In just two more weeks Maud would have been eighteen. It was funny — until that moment Sarah had never realized that young people could die.

That afternoon the captain gave orders for the *Tynemouth* to leave Port Stanley. As the ship moved out of the harbor Sarah stood at one of the murky portholes. For as long as she could see it, she watched the searchlight.

Chapter 15

Twenty four hours after leaving Port Stanley, the *Tynemouth* rounded the Cape and steamed into the Pacific.

Moments later, shouted orders could be heard echoing from on deck. Running feet pounded overhead.

Even through her aching emptiness, Sarah knew something was happening. Grabbing one of the latrine pails, even though it wasn't her day, she hurried up on deck to see what was going on.

A dozen sailors were scrambling up ladder ropes onto the tall wooden masts. Next moment they'd released the canvas that was lashed to the crossbars and sheets of sail fell free and swelled outward in the wind. The ship shot forward.

Sarah stared in fascination.

"It's quite a sight, isn't it?" Bea said, moving up beside her.

Sarah nodded, staring at the billowing sheets of sail. "Why didn't the captain use the sails before?"

"He was waiting to catch the Trade Winds. Now with luck they should carry us the rest of the way."

After two months of constant roaring from the steam screw, Sarah couldn't believe silence could be so wonderful. Then she noticed the sky. She'd grown used to seeing it a sooty grey color, bathed in constant billows of black smoke. For the first time it was a clear soft blue, and the floating clouds had golden edges where the sun touched them.

The golden edges blurred as Sarah's eyes filled with tears. She ached inside with the hurt of knowing Maud wasn't with her to see this. What made it worse was her guilt. If someone had to die it should have been her, not Maud. Her cousin hadn't even wanted to come, but she'd forced her to by reminding her of that promise to Uncle Tor.

Quickly she brushed at her eyes and turned away.

As day followed day, her guilt continued to grow. She had to find something else to think about. It was time they had another Dare, she decided, and this time she'd be the one to issue the challenge.

That evening after supper, when the girls were again lying listlessly in their bunks, she poked her head up and said carefully to Lizzie in the bunk above her, "I Dare you to go up on deck."

"Wot?" Lizzie had been half asleep.

"Go up on deck. Right now. I Dare you."

"Alone, or with you?" Lizzie's voice was cautious.

"With me, of course."

For a moment Lizzie didn't answer. Sarah wondered if she was still thinking of that man who had threatened her. Was she afraid to go up where she might bump into him? But he must have been bluffing with that threat to "fix her" — several weeks had passed and he'd done nothing. Besides, that had been before Maud's death. What had seemed important then didn't seem so important any longer.

"Go up on deck to do wot?" Lizzie asked warily.

"I haven't decided," Sarah returned evasively. She only knew that she had to strike back at Mrs. Worthing and Mr. Dubonnet, and going up on deck in defiance of orders was a way to do it. If they had allowed the girls to go ashore at Port Stanley Maud would still be alive. If they'd treated them decently — allowed them on deck in the sunshine — let them heat tea for Maud when Ruth Rhodes had asked . . .

"'Course I'll come. It's a Dare, ain't it?" The mischievous twinkle that had been missing for so long was back in Lizzie's green eyes.

Quietly they slipped out of their bunks and made their way through the shadowed compartment. Several of the other girls glanced up as they passed, but either lost interest when they ducked behind the curtain shielding the latrine pails, or didn't care enough to comment.

They started along the deck. When they reached the first bank of passenger cabins, they saw that the curtain on one of the windows had been pushed back. Sarah moved closer. Next moment tears welled up hot behind her eyelids, for on a table in the center of the cabin sat an African violet in a small pot.

"Wot's wrong?"

"Momma used to keep a violet in her bedroom. She said they were so brave and cheerful-looking they made her brave and cheerful too." Sarah brushed impatiently at her tears and deliberately made her voice casual. "When I was little, if ever I was scared or lonely I'd sneak into her room, and the smell of Momma's violets would make me feel better."

Before Sarah realized what she intended, Lizzie opened the cabin door, darted inside, picked up the violet and brought it outside.

"Lizzie! Put that back!"

"'Course I will." Lizzie looked offended. "I only brought it out so maybe it would make things better for us." She bent her head over the flowers.

Smiling, Sarah did the same.

"Better?" Lizzie asked after a moment.

Sarah nodded.

"Me too." Again Lizzie lowered her face into the flowers. "I never knew me mum," she said after a moment in a faraway voice. "But I bet she'd 'ave liked violets too."

Next moment she straightened, tossed her head as if to say she was just being silly, set the violet back inside the cabin exactly as it had been before, and rejoined Sarah. They continued around the deck.

But as they came back toward their stairs, they stopped in alarm. Not twenty feet away, a group of people were sitting on blankets. Mr. Dubonnet was among them.

Lizzie's face paled. "'Ere, into the cupboard," she whispered, pulling Sarah toward the storage locker.

They'd happened upon an informal deck party. Each person in turn had to entertain the others in some way — sing a song, tell a story.

The droning voices went on so long Sarah was almost asleep when something Mr. Dubonnet was reading caught her attention. She missed the poet's name and the first few lines, but though she didn't as a rule like poems, she liked what she heard of this one. Something about first robins and chattering squirrels. Uncle Tor must have read it to her sometime, for it seemed familiar.

At last people got to their feet, collected their blankets and moved away.

Sarah unwrapped herself from the storage locker. It hadn't been much of a strike back against Mrs. Worthing but at least they'd seen the violet. That helped a little. "We'd better go back," she told Lizzie.

By this time, Lizzie was unwinding herself from her hiding place as well. "'Oo'd want to spend an evening listening to all that dumb poetry?" she said, stretching to relax all the cramped spots.

Several days later rumors filtered down to the girls' compartment that the *Tynemouth* was to make another stop–over, this time at San Francisco. They'd stay three or four days to take on fresh water.

Surely they'd be allowed to go ashore this time, Sarah told herself, holding tight to her excitement, for everyone on board knew that Mr. Dubonnet's refusal to let the girls go ashore last time had resulted in Maud's death.

That night it was impossible to sleep.

Next day when the girls assembled for their daily walk, Mrs. Worthing called for attention. She announced the scheduled stop–over in San Francisco.

The girls waited expectantly.

"I understand from the crew who stayed on board during our stop–over at the Falkland Islands," Mrs. Worthing went on, "that you disobeyed orders and did not remain in your compartment." Her glance settled on Sarah. "As a result, one of your number caught pneumonia up on the cold deck and died."

Sarah was stunned. How could Mrs. Worthing say such a thing? It wasn't true! That wasn't why Maud had died. It had made her feel better to be up on deck in the fresh air and sunshine. But even as the thought registered, Sarah's anger changed to numbing uncertainty. Till that moment it had never occurred to her that the trips up on deck might have made Maud worse — that while the other girls improved, Maud had continued to grow sicker.

Had she been wrong to take her?

She pushed the thought away. No! Maud had wanted to go on deck. She'd have sickened even faster if she'd stayed below all that time.

But the doubt Mrs. Worthing had planted had taken root. Now Sarah remembered something her cousin had said one day when she'd started to get her ready. "I'll be fine staying down here today, Saree. You go up with the others and enjoy yourself."

She went trembly inside. She'd thought Maud had been trying to save her trouble. But what if her cousin really hadn't wanted to go? Was Mrs. Worthing right? Was it her fault that Maud had died?

The smothering blanket of guilt was so overwhelming that Sarah missed the next few words. Then Mrs. Worthing's voice again caught her attention.

". . . to make sure you are not tempted to disobey orders again and leave your quarters, a member of the crew will patrol the ship at all times." The talk was over. Beckoning to the girls to follow, Mrs. Worthing set off along the deck at a rapid pace.

They reached San Francisco the following day. The girls watched through the dirty portholes as again the rest of the passengers and most of the crewmen went ashore. Then, wrapped in their own private thoughts, they returned to their bunks.

Don't feel, Sarah told herself, but it was impossible. Think about something else. That was impossible too. What could she think about that would make her forget her guilt about Maud?

When the idea first struck she pushed it away, but it came back. The more she thought about it the more attractive it appeared. Going up on deck in defiance of orders wasn't enough any longer. Now she had to strike back at Mrs. Worthing personally, and she'd thought of just the way to do it.

She poked her head over the boards of the bunk above. "Remember those dresses we saw in Mrs. Worthing's closet?" She dropped her voice to a whisper that couldn't possibly carry to anyone else. "I'm going to put one of them on, and I Dare you to come with me and do the same."

Lizzie had been half asleep. At Sarah's whisper she turned and looked into the face just inches from hers. "Yer sure that's enough?"

Caution was forgotten. "No," Sarah replied, her heart pounding. She needed to prove that she and Lizzie could be as grand and fancy as Mrs. Worthing, if they were just given the chance. Mrs. Worthing would never know, of course, but she and Lizzie would, and that was all that mattered. For the rest of their lives no one would ever be able to take that knowledge away from them. "No. It isn't enough just to dress up," Sarah repeated. "After we've put on her clothes, I Dare us to promenade all the way around the deck."

Lizzie rolled onto her back, stretched, and stared at the bunk over her head. "Wot a good idea," she said brightly. "An' afterward we'll 'ave tea with them crew members wot are on duty to make sure we stay below."

"Does that mean you're scared?"

"'Course I'm scared."

"You refuse?"

"'Oo said anything about refusing?" For a minute longer Lizzie continued staring at the boards of the bunk above, then she sat up and swung her feet to the floor. "Only first we've got to find out 'ow often them crew members patrol the deck, an' 'ow long between rounds they stay below, so when we do our fancy promenade they won't see us." Pushing past Sarah, she led the way up their darkened stairs. Pausing just long enough to make sure the way was clear, she crossed the small area of deck to the storage locker. Climbing in, she made room for Sarah.

Not more than ten or fifteen minutes after they were safely out of sight, a crewman appeared. He made a complete circle down one side of the deck then back up the other before disappearing back to the crew's quarters below. Fifteen minutes later another crewman did the same. Then a half hour passed before the next deck check.

After that, the girls waited shivering in their hiding place for over an hour till they heard the clock in the wheelhouse chime eleven, but no more crewman came up on deck at all.

"By tomorrow they'll probably 'ave stopped

checkin' altogether," Lizzie said, crawling stiffly out of the locker and starting back below.

"Maybe, but we're not going to risk it," Sarah replied. "We'll wait till we hear the clock chime ten." That would be their second day in port. Bea had said they'd be here for at least three days and possibly four.

Next night, the girls waited impatiently as the rest of the compartment settled into sleep. They continued to wait. Finally, when they were sure it was ten o'clock and the ship was silent, they slipped out the door at the top of their stairs and crept soundlessly to Mrs. Worthing's stateroom.

The door was locked.

"So much fer that," Lizzie said, turning back.

Sarah caught her arm. "You'll have to pick it."

"Wot?"

"You told me you could pick locks."

"So I kin, but if I do an' we get caught, we'll be in trouble."

"I don't care."

"Maybe you don't, but I do. 'Cos I'll be the one wot gets locked up."

"Please, Lizzie?" She couldn't lamely give up and go back below. She had to do something to strike back at Mrs. Worthing. Not just for her own sake but for Maud's. Sarah took a deep breath. "I Dare you to pick the lock," she said deliberately.

For a moment, Lizzie looked disbelieving, then her resistance faded — a person couldn't refuse a Dare. Moving back to the cabin, she bent down beside the door and examined the lock, then turned her attention to the floor. She found what she was looking for — a long thin splinter of wood. Gently she twisted the wood splinter in the lock. A moment later the door swung open.

"Quick! Inside!" Sarah whispered, leading the way.

"You want to dress up first?" Lizzie asked, closing the door. "I'll stand by the window an' watch in case one of them crewmen comes around."

But Sarah had left caution behind. "The crewman aren't going to come around." She'd spotted the brown calf-leather boots, the ones Lizzie had fallen in love with that day on deck. They were sitting beside the bed as if Mrs. Worthing had just taken them off. "While you put on those boots and that yellow dress, I'm going to put on that blue one."

"Someone should keep watch —" Lizzie began.

"If we don't dress up together, how can we walk around the deck? Besides," Sarah added, feeling like giggling for the first time in weeks, "if someone comes along, we'll do what you said that first night — we'll act as if we belong here — as if Mrs. Worthing gave us permission."

"As if anyone wud believe that." But the excitement was contagious. Moving toward the clothes closet, Lizzie reached for the yellow dress.

Sarah meantime was putting on the blue one. She'd need a crinoline, she decided. Rummaging through the closet she chose the fullest one she could find. She'd never seen one as fancy as this before.

By this time Lizzie had finished putting on the yellow dress and turned her attention to the boots. "'Ow does a person do up all them buttons?"

"With a button hook. Look in there." Sarah nodded vaguely toward a chest of drawers, for her attention was on the crinoline.

Lizzie opened each drawer in turn. The button hook lay in the bottom one. She picked it up and was just about to shut the drawer when her breath caught in excitement. "Cor! Look at this!" She lifted out a glass-topped jewel box. Shining through the glass could be seen a pearl necklace, a gold signet ring, a cameo on a chain, and a gleaming ruby pendant. "Cor!" she said again.

The jewel box, like the cabin door, was locked.

"Open it!" Sarah urged.

"I wudn't dare. Think wot'd 'appen if we wos caught."

"How could we get caught? It isn't as if we're going to take anything. I just want to be able to see the jewelry properly without all that glass in the way. Then you can lock it right up again."

Lizzie hesitated a moment longer, then she studied the lock. Next second the jewel box was open.

The promise just to look was forgotten. Reverently, Sarah lifted out the pearl necklace.

Lizzie meantime picked up the ruby pendant and fastened it around her neck. Reaching for the hand mirror on top of the dresser she gazed at herself in awe. "I never knew I cud be so grand." Her fingers touched the ruby pendant lovingly. "If this wos mine I'd never take it off — not even at night. I'd keep it on even under me night clothes."

"We'll wear the jewelry when we walk around the deck," Sarah said impulsively.

Lizzie was too much in love with the ruby pendant to argue.

They eased open the stateroom door. The deck was deserted. Stepping outside, they exchanged one quick nervous glance, then proceeded to walk leisurely around the deck as if they were the most famous and important passengers who had ever sailed on the *Tynemouth*.

Twenty minutes later they were back at Mrs. Worthing's stateroom. They slipped inside and closed the door. Next moment both of them dissolved in giggles.

"We did it!" Sarah exclaimed delightedly.

"Let's go again!" Lizzie suggested.

Sarah was about to agree when a sound outside the window caught her attention. "Shhh!" she whispered. Heart pounding, she edged back the curtain and peered out.

The deck outside was as quiet and deserted as it had been before. But the scare had spoiled her excitement. "We'd better not go again," she told Lizzie quietly.

Unfastening the pearl necklace, she put it carefully back in the jewel box. Then taking off the blue dress and crinoline, she returned them to the closet and dressed again in her dreary gingham uniform. Lizzie meantime was struggling with the buttons on the brown leather boots.

For some reason Sarah was uneasy. "Hurry," she said.

At last Lizzie had them undone.

"I'll put your things away while you get dressed," Sarah told her, eager to save time. "Don't forget to take off that pendant."

By the time Sarah had returned the yellow dress to the closet, the boots to the side of the bed, the looking glass and the jewel box to the chest of drawers and had tidied everything, Lizzie was again in her uniform.

"Ready?" Sarah asked, moving toward the door.

They slipped outside, reset the lock and eased the door closed behind them.

The deck was still deserted.

Sarah let her breath out in a long sigh. "That was fun."

"It were the most wonderful night in my entire life," Lizzie answered softly.

Chapter 16

The following morning, as Sarah and Lizzie were dumping the latrine pails, a tug left the dock and headed for the ship. Were some of the passengers returning early? If so, they'd run their Dare just in time.

"Crew members most likely," Lizzie suggested. "We'd better not let 'em see us out 'ere."

"It's all right when we're dumping pails," Sarah insisted, but Lizzie was already scuttling across the deck toward the stairs back to their compartment.

Laughing at Lizzie for being so timid, Sarah followed. But when she reached the safety of their stairs, she turned back to watch. Two men got out of the tug and reboarded the *Tynemouth* — Mr. Dubonnet, rotund and heavy set, the Captain, tall and spare. Sarah watched them cross the deck, pass her hiding place, then continue toward the passenger cabins. For some reason she felt a nudge of uneasiness.

"'Oo is it?" Lizzie whispered from the bottom of the stairs.

Sarah told her.

"Why wud they come back? D'you think somebody saw —"

"Shhhh," Sarah warned sharply. Taking the steps in large strides, she moved past Lizzie into their compartment. She was sure no one had seen them last night, but just the same, it would be best if none of the other girls knew anything about it.

They put the latrine buckets behind the makeshift curtain and had just returned to their bunks when footsteps sounded on the stairs. Next moment Mr. Dubonnet, Captain McLaughlin and an accompanying seaman burst into the compartment.

For a moment, Mr. Dubonnet looked around in silence, then he located Lizzie. He pointed. "That is the girl."

Captain McLaughlin moved in long–legged strides toward Lizzie's bunk. Seizing her carpetbag, he dumped the contents onto the bed.

White faced and trembling, Lizzie looked over at Sarah.

One of the crew must have seen them last night after all, Sarah realized, and sent word ashore. But what was the captain looking for? True, they'd put on Mrs. Worthing's clothes, but they hadn't taken anything!

The search of the carpetbag revealed nothing.

"Look in the blankets," Dubonnet directed, "or better still, let me." Shouldering the captain out of the way, he leaned into Lizzie's bunk. Seconds later, he pulled his hand out from under the blanket and turned to face them with the ruby pendant dangling from his fingers.

There was an audible gasp from the other girls who were watching in fascination from their bunks. But Lizzie and Sarah were too numb to make a sound.

"You rotten little thief," Dubonnet said softly to Lizzie.

She backed away in horror. "I didn't snitch that! Somebody else must 'ave put it there." She turned an ashen face to Sarah. "Tell 'em I didn't snitch it," she begged.

But Sarah remained silent. She'd been too busy putting things away the night before to notice what Lizzie was doing. She thought Lizzie had put the pendant back into the jewel box but she hadn't seen her do so. "*If it wos mine I'd never take it off, not even at night time. I'd keep it on even under me night clothes. . .*" Had she been still wearing it under her uniform?

Into Sarah's mind rushed a memory of the carpetbag that first morning on the dock, and of all Maud's warnings. ". . . *shouldn't make too good a friend . . . unpredictable and undisciplined . . . lead you into trouble . . .*"

"Bring these girls to my quarters." McLaughlin's stern voice broke into Sarah's jumbled thoughts.

Next second, the crewman who had accompanied the captain took each of them by an arm. He propelled them past the fascinated audience in the other bunks and up the stairs.

More than an hour later Sarah returned alone to the crowded below decks compartment.

"Wot happened? Where's Lizzie? Did she really steal that jewelry?" Questions flew.

Sarah climbed into her bunk and turned her face to the wall.

If she'd had a chance to talk privately to Lizzie it would have been different, she told herself. But the captain had refused to let them have even a moment together.

First, Mr. Dubonnet had thrown questions at both of them. Had they gone into Mrs. Worthing's stateroom? Yes. Had they put on her clothes? Yes. Didn't they know they'd been given express orders not to leave their compartment? Yes.

Then he'd focused on Lizzie. Did she steal that pendant? No.

Did she put it on? Yes.

Did she like it? Yes, but she hadn't —

"Just answer the questions. My sister tells me that her stateroom door is always kept locked . . ." Lizzie blanched as she realized where the questions were leading ". . . So how did you get in?"

Lizzie turned to Sarah, silently begging her to share the responsibility and admit that she'd urged her to pick those locks. But Sarah continued to remain silent.

"Answer the question! How did you get in?"

Lizzie turned back to Mr. Dubonnet. For the first time her eyes were dark with fear. "I picked the lock," she admitted in a low voice.

Sarah caught the glimmer of satisfaction that crossed Dubonnet's face. It was almost as if he wanted her to be guilty. "Mrs. Worthing tells me she also keeps her jewel case locked. Did you pick that lock too?"

Lizzie waited only a moment this time before answering. "Yes." Her voice wasn't quite steady and the fear in her eyes had been joined by hurt and disillusionment.

It was the captain's turn to ask questions. He'd heard rumors that Lizzie had been a child pickpocket. Was it true?

"Yes," Lizzie said again, but she insisted she hadn't taken the pendant. She'd worn it for a bit but then she'd taken if off and put it back in the jewel box.

The captain didn't believe her. "You will be kept in confinement on board ship until we reach Victoria." He nodded to the crewman to come forward and take her away.

For the third time, Lizzie turned and looked over at Sarah. Lifting her chin as she had that first night on deck, she said quietly, "Wot kin you expect from a day wot starts with dumpin' latrine pails?"

Next moment she had been conducted away.

Long after the other girls were asleep, Sarah lay staring into the darkness. She didn't dare close her eyes, for she knew imprinted against the inside of the lids would be an image of the hurt and accusation she'd seen on Lizzie's face.

If only she'd had a chance to explain to Lizzie why she hadn't admitted her share in things. What good would it have done? It would just have plunged her into trouble too, and for no purpose. She hadn't taken the pendant. She'd had nothing to do with it.

She should never have suggested going near Mrs. Worthing's cabin. She should have known Lizzie would be tempted to take something. After all, she'd watched her search that carpetbag the first morning. Lizzie had even been planning to steal that blue shawl. She'd admitted it honestly —

Unbidden, the memory of that evening swept back. *"You're my friend,"* Lizzie had said. *"Didn't you know I'd always tell you the truth?"*

The same hurt and disillusionment that had shone in her eyes that evening had been there again this morning.

Sarah felt a huge empty hole open up somewhere deep inside. Maybe Maud had been right about Lizzie being unpredictable and undisciplined, but Lizzie didn't lie. She hadn't lied about that blue shawl. She hadn't lied the day on the quay about looking for something to steal from the carpetbag. She didn't lie this morning when Mr. Dubonnet asked how she'd opened the locks on the cabin door and the jewel box, and she didn't lie when the captain asked if she'd been a pickpocket.

Then why had Sarah been so quick to assume she'd been lying about not taking the pendant?

If Sarah had trusted her and spoken up for her and insisted Lizzie must be innocent, the captain might have listened. Instead, she'd made it plain that she suspected Lizzie too.

Penelope was making a lump under the blanket. Angrily, Sarah pulled her out. Reaching for her carpetbag, she tossed the doll inside, buried her under the extra shift and the apron she never wore, then pushed the bag out of sight to the far end of the bunk.

She was a long time falling asleep.

Chapter 17

Next morning Sarah had no wish to face either Mr. Dubonnet or Mrs. Worthing — not when they knew she'd been the other girl in the dress–up scheme. So when the others went up on deck she pretended to be ill.

Word came from Mrs. Worthing that she was to come up on deck immediately.

Sarah ignored the summons. She remained in her bunk sick with self-loathing. Everything was her fault. She'd forced Maud to come on this awful journey and now Maud was dead. She'd forced Lizzie to pick those locks and Lizzie had been arrested. When she should have insisted Lizzie was innocent and shared the blame about the locks, she'd thought only of herself.

The carpetbag was making an uncomfortable

lump against her feet. Angrily, she kicked at it. At least she'd had the sense to get rid of that foolish doll. She would also get rid of those foolish dreams about life being an adventure, she promised herself, for dreams and dolls were for children. In the last little while she'd grown up.

"Mrs. Worthing says you're to come up on deck right now!" Arabella announced breathlessly, flinging open the door of the compartment.

Reluctantly Sarah got to her feet.

She emerged on deck to find both Mr. Dubonnet and Mrs. Worthing waiting, together with all the other girls and most of the governesses — not only the eight who had traveled with them but most of the others as well. Everyone was staring. From their expressions it was clear they knew about the stolen pendant and about Lizzie being arrested. Were they wondering what part she'd played? Sarah wondered. Quickly she focused her attention on the deck.

"I've asked you to assemble here this morning," Mr. Dubonnet began, "because we'll be arriving in Victoria in just five more days." He tugged at the bottom of his waistcoat as if hoping to stretch it to meet his trousers and turned to the assembled governesses. "Before then we must clarify your situation. I know many of you have come on this voyage hoping to find work in —"

"Not many of us — all," Ruth Rhodes corrected.

". . . in your present profession," Dubonnet went on as if she hadn't spoken, "but unfortunately there aren't as many jobs available as we originally thought. So, if you will agree to be brides instead —"

A dozen voices lifted in protest.

"I'm afraid you will have little choice," Dubonnet told them bluntly.

The protests swelled.

Among the drab brown and grey dresses, Dubonnet caught sight of Bea's bright green one with its daring neckline. "Ah, Miss — Miss O'Toole!" he said in relief, checking his list. "I'm sure *you'd* rather be a bride than a governess."

Bea gave him an amused stare. She repositioned her parasol so the sun wasn't on her face and said blandly, "Mrs., not Miss, and I rather think I'll go into business on my own."

"I suggest you reconsider, Mrs. O'Toole." Dubonnet's tone was condescending. "Running a successful business is a challenge even for a man and quite beyond the experience of any woman."

"Doesn't that depend on the kind of business?" Bea's eyebrows lifted innocently. "For the one I plan to run, I assure you I have had lots of experience."

Dubonnet's eyes flashed angrily. For a moment he seemed on the point of a biting retort. Then he must have remembered his position for his mouth set in a firm line and he turned away. His glance fell on Mary. "You, at least, I will put down as a bride," he stated coldly, "for you're much too young to be a governess." He stared at the birthmark. "Though perhaps on second thought . . ."

The color drained from Mary's cheeks.

For a minute longer Dubonnet stared, then to Sarah's relief his gaze moved on. "Now for you, young ladies." His smug self–assurance was back in place. "As soon as we dock, you will be meeting your future husbands, which I know you are eager to do. Within a day or two, all of you can expect to be married. All of you except one, that is." His voice turned silky, and his glance moved along the rows of gingham-clad figures till it reached Sarah. "One girl will have to be patient for a week or so . . ."

He was talking about her, Sarah realized in horror. What did he have planned?

". . . for she is to be the bride of a man from a remote region," he was spacing the words carefully, "who does not wish to come down to claim her until everyone else has gone."

Everyone could see who Mr. Dubonnet was looking at. They turned to stare, *Why doesn't he want to be seen*? was clearly written on their faces.

Sarah turned cold with terror. Was this her punishment for dressing up in Mrs. Worthing's clothes — to be married off to some man who didn't even want to be seen, then taken to some deserted place? No wonder Mrs. Worthing had insisted she come up on deck, so Mr. Dubonnet could enjoy her panic when she realized what he was planning!

Well, at least she could deny him that satisfaction. Keeping her face expressionless, she met his gaze calmly for a minute, then leisurely looked away.

If Dubonnet was disappointed, he gave no sign. Nodding to his sister, he indicated that the talk was over and that she should start the walk.

Still too numb to feel anything, Sarah fell in with the others.

As always, conversation was kept to whispered undertones while they were on deck, but the moment the girls returned to their compartment everyone started talking at once.

"What will they be like?"

"Do we get to choose?"

"How soon will the marriages take place?"

"Wot if we don't like any of them?"

"If they haven't had womenfolk around for a l–l–long time, d'you think they'll try to hug us, or k–k–kiss us right off?" Fanny asked, sitting down on the edge of her bunk. Embarrassment brought a touch of pink to her usually pale cheeks.

"I'm sure there will be no hugging or kissing until long after you are married," Ruth Rhodes said calmly. "After all, these are civilized men."

Arabella giggled. "Not that civilized, I hope. After this trip I could do with some hugging and kissing."

"Wot about after the wedding?" someone said. "Wot if we don't like who we've bin given to?"

"Or what if we do?" a soft voice took over.

"What if we do like him only we don't know what to do?"

Sarah closed her ears to block out their questions. She was terrified — not only for herself, but for the others as well. How many of them, she wondered, would end up like Momma?

Chapter 18

By next morning, Sarah could feel her panic building. In four more days the *Tynemouth* would reach Victoria. In four more days she would be put away somewhere to wait for that man Mr. Dubonnet had chosen to be her husband, and Lizzie would be handed over to the authorities. She knew it was too late to change what was going to happen to her, but somehow she must find a way to help her friend.

If only she could find out who had taken the pendant, for she was sure now that Lizzie hadn't.

It couldn't have been one of the passengers, she decided. As soon as they'd all gone ashore, the ship had moved back out into the middle of the harbor and dropped anchor. If any passengers had wanted to come back on board they'd have had to come by tug. And no tug had arrived except the one this morning.

Then could it have been one of the other girls? The likeliest suspect was Arabella. She'd followed them up on deck the night Lizzie found that shawl and could have followed them again. Perhaps she saw them dressing up, then, when they went back below, crept into Mrs. Worthing's cabin and stole the pendant.

But how would she have got in? Sarah distinctly remembered relocking the cabin door. She'd even tested it. Arabella couldn't pick locks and neither could any of the other girls.

That left the crew. Had it been the man she'd seen leaving their compartment several weeks ago? If only she'd got a look at his face! Sarah's mind was racing. She was sure now the man had stolen Fanny's brooch and Maud's book, and probably their food — so why not the pendant, too? Maybe he'd made a late patrol around the deck the night before and saw them dressing up in Mrs. Worthing's cabin. There had to be a set of master keys on board somewhere, in case of emergencies. The crew would know about them. Maybe the man got the key, waited till she and Lizzie had gone back below, then helped himself to the pendant he'd seen Lizzie wearing, intending to blame the theft on them.

But why hide the stolen jewelry in Lizzie's bunk? Why not keep it? Why would he want to fix it so it would look as if some unknown orphan had —

Fix it! Those were the words Lizzie had used

about the man she'd gone up to meet — "'*e said I wud make trouble, an' 'e'd 'ave to fix it so I cudn't.*"

Forcing down her excitement, Sarah tried to think. If only Lizzie had told her who it was, but she'd refused. "*If I tell you 'e'll just 'ave it in for you too.*"

Remembering that made her feel even more guilty.

She pushed the thought away and tried to concentrate. If Lizzie had been able to work out who'd stolen their things, then she should be able to as well, Sarah told herself.

She started back at the beginning and tried to remember everything that had happened. First, the morning when they'd started out. She could still picture the smile on her cousin's face when Harley came to see them off and gave her that book of his poems. She could still see the light that had shone in Maud's eyes as he'd read that one poem aloud — something about spring —

That was the poem she'd heard being read the night of the deck party! No wonder it had seemed familiar!

It was as if Sarah's thoughts were colored shapes in a kaleidoscope. Adding that new one shook all the others into disarray. As they resettled, they formed an entirely new pattern — a frightening new pattern.

Sarah knew who Lizzie had gone up on deck to meet and who had stolen the pendant. She also knew why it had been hidden in Lizzie's bunk.

It was her turn to be frightened.

Chapter 19

Sarah's first thought next morning was that there were now only three days left. Her second was that she had to tell Bea what she'd discovered in case something went wrong. But it wasn't her day on pail duty. That meant she'd have to find a way to talk to Bea during their walk.

However, Mrs. Worthing made that impossible. She hardly took her eyes off Sarah all the time they were on deck. Then, as soon as the walk was over, she settled down in a deck chair within sight of their stairway. Sarah had no choice but to spend the day lying in her bunk, staring at Lizzie's empty space above her head and counting the hours until tomorrow.

Now there were two days left. Even before breakfast, Sarah was on deck, for this *was* her day on pail duty. To her relief, Bea was up early too, standing by the rail, gazing out over the cresting waves. Sarah hurried toward her. For several moments she talked without interruption in a voice pitched too low to carry to anyone else.

As Bea listened her sunny smile changed to a frown. "Are you sure?" she asked when Sarah ran out of words.

Sarah nodded. "But I'll need proof if I hope to clear Lizzie."

"Then you'll need a key. Wait here." Less than five minutes later Bea was back. She slipped a metal key into Sarah's hand. "I borrowed it from Ned," she said, as if that explained everything.

All the rest of the day Sarah stayed below trying to be patient. When evening finally came and the governesses went up on deck, she followed, the key Bea had given her carefully hidden in her hand. From the safety of the storage locker she watched the passengers drift lazily toward the dining salon. When the last of them disappeared she left her hiding place. Half an hour later she was safely back in their shadowed compartment.

Next morning she went on deck again. Since this was their last full day before docking, perhaps Mrs. Worthing would be too busy to bother policing them.

"Did you find what you were looking for?" Bea asked as Sarah returned the key.

Sarah nodded. Her lips felt tight. "But what

if the captain won't let me talk to him?" That thought had kept her awake a good part of the night.

"He will if I ask him to." A twinkle came into Bea's eyes. "He and I are quite good friends."

In spite of her worries, Sarah smiled.

Bea took Sarah to the wheelhouse, introduced her to the captain, then left them alone together.

McLaughlin listened in silence. When Sarah finally finished speaking, he said curtly, "You must make such accusations directly to the man you are accusing, and offer him the chance to defend himself."

Sarah lifted frightened eyes to his face, but the captain was already moving away. Motioning to Sarah to follow, he crossed the deck toward the cabin Sarah had visited the previous evening.

Since the night before she'd been rehearsing what she would say, but as the door opened in reply to Captain McLaughlin's knock, the words refused to come.

For a moment the silence dragged on, then in a bored voice Dubonnet drawled, "Is someone going to tell me what this is about?"

Never before had Sarah needed Maud so badly — or Lizzie — or Bea. She couldn't face this man all by herself — not when he was so clever with words, and so experienced in handling other people.

McLaughlin cleared his throat. "This girl has come to me with what I must admit sounds like a ridiculous accusation. I have brought her to you to determine the truth."

"I see." Raising his monocle, Dubonnet studied Sarah.

She wished she could sit down. Her head was buzzing and she'd started to feel sick. She'd tell them she'd made a mistake and escape back below, she decided, for the captain was right. These were ridiculous accusations. Lizzie would understand. It was crazy even to think that she could accuse a man like this of —

"I'm afraid I cannot waste any more of my time," Dubonnet's bored voice broke the silence, "waiting for an uneducated orphan girl to decide whether or not —"

Sarah's fear was forgotten. Raising her eyes she met his squarely. "I've come to accuse you of stealing." Her voice was low but clearly audible. "I accuse you of stealing food and personal things from the girls you were supposed to be looking after. Lizzie knew you were the thief, so to keep her quiet you set a trap. When you heard that someone had been in Mrs. Worthing's cabin dressing up in her clothes, you came back and pretended to check to see if anything had been taken. Then you stole Mrs. Worthing's pendant yourself and hid it in Lizzie's bunk so she'd be arrested." By now her voice was shaking so badly it was hard to get enough breath to speak.

Instead of being angry, Dubonnet seemed amused. He brushed at a bit of fluff on his coat sleeve. "How odd that no one should have noticed me skulking about in your small storage compartment, hiding ruby pendants in people's bunks and helping myself to your food and treasures." The sarcasm in his tone was biting.

An amused chuckle came from the captain.

Rather than frightening Sarah further, Dubonnet's sarcasm made her more determined. Again she lifted her eyes to meet his. "You could have come in any morning when we were on deck," she told him bluntly, "particularly on the days you sent word down that no one was allowed to stay below. If anyone saw you and wondered why you were there you could pretend to be checking on something."

Dubonnet continued to smile, but the smile no longer reached his eyes. He turned to the captain. "As you must know, there is no truth in any of this. I suggest this girl apologize to me, then return to her quarters."

"Lizzie told you she wouldn't make trouble," Sarah rushed on. "She just wanted to clear her name with the other girls. But you didn't believe her. You said you'd have to find a way to fix it so she couldn't make trouble."

"Nonsense!" A flash of anger lit Dubonnet's eyes. He'd been unprepared to hear his own words thrown back at him. But next second he had himself back under control. He turned again to the captain and said in a silky voice, "Of course this is nonsense, but in case you should be tempted to waste time looking into it, I suggest you reconsider. Your employer would hardly appreciate having his company plunged into an expensive slander action on the word of an uneducated orphan girl." He coughed apologetically. "I'm sure you agree that I couldn't allow such lies to go unchallenged."

McLaughlin's expression changed. He was going to back down, Sarah realized with horror.

"I can prove it!" she cried. Before either man realized what she was intending, she darted across the small cabin, opened the top drawer of the desk under the window and brought out what she'd found hidden there the previous evening — Maud's book of poems and Fanny's brooch.

The shock on the captain's face was obvious.

For a moment Sarah thought he might support her after all, but Dubonnet's eyes were blazing. "How clever of you to think of planting these things in my quarters," he said bitingly. "But I'm sure the captain realizes his employer would not be impressed by a man who could be taken in by such a ruse."

In the face of such a blatant threat, McLaughlin's glance fell. "Yes. Well . . . as you say, there's no point in upsetting my employer," he told Dubonnet. He was avoiding Sarah's eyes completely. "Perhaps we can settle this between ourselves. The pendant has already been returned to Mrs. Worthing. We can let this girl return the brooch and poetry book to their rightful owners, and that will just leave the question of what to do with the girl in confinement. If you agree that the charges against her might be dropped, I think this whole unfortunate affair can be forgotten."

Sarah felt sick and trembly. She'd failed. It had all been for nothing. Lizzie's name would never be cleared — Dubonnet would see to that. And they'd never escape him. He'd find a way to silence both of them so neither could ever again try to speak out. That's why she was to be married off to that man who was going to take her far away from anyone. Now Dubonnet would arrange something even worse for Lizzie.

Numbly, she accepted the book and the brooch from the captain and returned to the below decks compartment. As she passed Fanny's bunk she dropped the brooch into her hand.

"Oh!" Fanny exclaimed. "Oh!" Her fingers tightened around the piece of jewelry and her eyes filled with tears.

Sarah didn't stop to explain. She was afraid if she did the whole story would come tumbling out — then she and Lizzie would be in even more trouble. Crawling into her own bunk, she opened Maud's book to the poem her cousin had loved so dearly —

You'll not be with me when the spring is here,
But I'll remember other happier springs
When distance did not part us. I will hear
The sky awakening call of the first robin,
The foolish squirrels chattering in the trees.
Wherever you are you will hear them also,
And in sharing we will once again be joined.

When Lizzie appeared on the stairs a few minutes later gasps of surprise came from the other girls, followed by a flood of questions.

Lizzie ignored both the questions and the surprise. Crossing the compartment, she climbed into the bunk over Sarah's head.

For a moment neither of them spoke. Then Lizzie said softly, "I 'eard wot you did. Captain told me."

"It didn't do any good," Sarah told her bitterly. "They're going to cover everything up."

"You tried. That's wot's important."

"I made things worse. He's going to punish us."

"So? 'Ow does that make 'im different from Matron?"

"Don't you see? He can't take a chance on letting us tell anybody else what we've discovered." Dropping her voice so Lizzie had to strain to hear, Sarah told her about the man she was to be married to who wouldn't even come to claim her until he was sure he wouldn't be seen. "He'll plan something even worse for you."

"Why won't 'e be seen?"

In spite of the closeness of the crowded compartment, Sarah shivered. "I don't know."

For a long moment Lizzie was silent. When she spoke again she changed the subject. "'Ow did you work out it wos 'im?"

With relief, Sarah pulled her thoughts away from her future husband. "I kept thinking about that poem he'd read on deck that sounded so familiar. It seemed strange that a man like him would enjoy poetry. Then I remembered where I'd heard it before. It was in Maud's book — the one that was stolen." She paused, then added softly, "It was her favorite poem." A lump came into her throat. Swallowing hard to dislodge it, she forced her voice to sound normal. "Is that how you knew too?"

Lizzie shook her head. "It wos when we saw that fire in Mrs. Worthing's stateroom. She said 'er brother often came up in the evenings, bringing a little extra tea an' oatmeal and fixin' somethin' to eat. I wondered if it wos our tea an' porridge wot 'e wos eating. Then one night when I wos in that storage cupboard I 'eard 'im trying to sell Fanny's brooch to one of the passengers, only nobody'd buy it."

"Was it awful where they had you locked up?" Sarah asked in a small voice.

"It weren't my favorite place," Lizzie replied.

Again for a moment there was silence, then in a completely different voice Lizzie said, "'E must of bin 'olding the pendant 'idden in 'is hand that morning. As soon as 'e knew wot bunk wos mine 'e pretended to find it in the blanket."

"I should have spoken up," Sarah told her softly.

"So, you spoke up today — that wos 'arder."

Sarah settled back in her bunk. After a moment, she leaned down and retrieved her carpetbag. Pushing aside the extra shift and the unused apron, she brought Penelope back out. Perhaps she wasn't too old for rag dolls after all — or for dreams.

Chapter 20

All evening, whispers swept the below decks compartment. Was Lizzie guilty or innocent? Then the question sank into unimportance, for early next morning through the tiny portholes the girls could see land in the distance.

Hourly, as the faint line on the horizon grew larger, the excitement grew. Even the prospect of being married off to a stranger couldn't dim the joy of finally getting off this ship.

On the morning of the 17th of September, ninety–one days after it had left London, the *Tynemouth* sailed into Esquimalt harbor. The girls were packed and waiting, closed carpetbags at the foot of every bunk. Perhaps not quite as bulging as when they'd started out, Sarah found herself thinking, for many of their meager garments had worn out during the voyage.

The first class passengers were already on deck, positioned along the rail, watching the shoreline swim closer. But the orphanage girls remained below for they were going to Victoria. "The *Tynemouth*, because of its size, cannot sail over the sandbar that sits at the entrance to Victoria Harbor," Mrs. Worthing had explained the previous day. "That is why it will dock at Esquimalt, a few miles away. That is where all the rest of the passengers will get off. But because you are going to Victoria, you will wait on board for a small naval boat to take you the last few miles. Until it arrives you will stay in your quarters."

The seven governesses had gone up on deck with the passengers. Mary remained with the girls.

They watched through the tiny portholes as people swarmed ashore, some laughing, some crying, but all thankful to be safely back on land.

Sarah was looking for Bea. At last she located her, moving across the deck, dressed in brilliant pink as she'd been that first day. When she reached the gangplank she paused, looked back and waved.

Sarah knew Bea wouldn't be able to see her behind the tiny circle of dirty glass, but she waved back anyway. Next moment a surge of passengers swept Bea from sight and Sarah felt an empty hole open up somewhere deep inside.

The girls continued to wait. After an hour they left the portholes and sat back down on their bunks. But they kept their bonnets on and their carpetbags in their hands. By early afternoon the bonnets had been discarded and the luggage set down. By late afternoon, the eagerness on the girls' faces had changed to confusion and disappointment.

It was not until forty-eight hours later that a small naval boat drew alongside. Half a dozen grinning sailors handed the girls one at a time down onto the deck of the tug. It took some maneuvering, for by now the wind had come up and the water was rough. When it was Arabella's turn she managed to lose her balance and one of the sailors had to catch her.

When all the girls were finally aboard, the boat started along the few miles of open water to Victoria. Sarah watched impatiently as the distant shoreline drew closer. How would it feel to have solid land under her feet again, instead of the constantly rocking water? How would it feel to smell grass and trees — to hear the birds . . .

Her throat closed in rising panic, for what she'd thought from a distance to be crates and boxes on the shoreline turned out to be groups of men — upwards of three hundred of them. As the tug bumped softly against the dock, the men pressed closer.

Arabella giggled.

Many of the girls were pushing to be first onto the wharf, but Sarah struggled to stay back. However, the crowd pushed from behind and she was swept up with the others. Next moment they were all surrounded by the milling men.

At last, to Sarah's relief, Mr. Dubonnet pushed his way through and ordered the girls to follow. But the crowd moved with them. As they tried to make their way two by two along the quay and onto the street, hands reached out to touch them.

Someone started to cry.

By now the crowd had swelled to more than five hundred.

"I don't know as wot we wos better off on that ship," Lizzie said in a frightened voice.

Sarah couldn't even answer. Don't panic, she told herself. It was sure to end soon.

At last they reached the Marine Barracks which had been temporarily cleared of military personnel in order to house them.

It could have been the *Tynemouth* all over again. Upstairs was a large meeting room; their sleeping quarters were down below — the same hard cots, the same grubby grey blankets, the same hopelessly small fly–specked windows. Even the latrine buckets were the same. The only difference was that the floor wasn't rolling.

The following morning, more terrified than she'd ever been before, Sarah joined Lizzie and the other girls on the rows of chairs set out in the large hall to wait for their prospective bride-grooms.

"Your friend Bea O'Toole said we shouldn't worry, cos men wos easy to 'andle," Lizzie said in a tight, funny voice, pleating the hem of her uniform nervously. "She said it was just a case of learning 'ow."

Sarah felt a wave of longing for Bea's unquenchable optimism. If only she were here. "When did she say that?"

"When she wos lookin' for you on deck that last day, only you'd gone down for another pail. She said she couldn't wait, so wud I tell you for her. Only I forgot."

"Did she say anything else?"

"Something about Penny somethin'–or–other."

For the first time in days, Sarah's spirits lifted. "What was it?" she asked eagerly.

"I can't remember."

"Lizzie, it's important! You've got to remember."

"I can't, cos I didn't listen." Lizzie's distress was reflected in her face. "I didn't figure it mattered cos I didn't know 'oo that person wos."

Sarah tried to cover her disappointment. Nothing would be gained by making Lizzie feel awful. But deep inside she ached with the emptiness of not knowing what Bea's message had been.

Next moment even that was forgotten, as the doors at the end of the hall opened. A crowd of men started to file through, eagerly studying the rows of waiting girls as they crossed the floor.

Sarah went cold and shaky inside. Quickly she glanced at Lizzie and saw her own terror reflected on Lizzie's thin face. In another few seconds, the men would be on them —

"I thought I made it clear last evening," Mr. Dubonnet's angry voice sounded behind them, "that arrangements have already been made concerning the men you two will marry."

Pushing through the chairs he came around in front of them.

"Your husband," he told Lizzie, his voice smug and satisfied, "will arrive first thing tomorrow morning. Yours," his glance shifted to Sarah, "will be here to claim you before the week is out. Until then, both of you are to remain in your quarters."

At his use of the term "claim," Sarah felt a new surge of fear. But that wouldn't be for several days yet, she reminded herself. For the time being anything was better than remaining here to be ogled by a crowd of strangers. Almost with relief she got to her feet.

Lizzie started to follow. But Dubonnet moved just enough so he was leaning over her, peering down. Lizzie couldn't get to her feet without brushing against him. She sank back in her chair.

A gleam of satisfaction came into Dubonnet's eyes as he saw her discomfort. In a silky, smug tone he continued, "I should warn you, my dear, that the man you are going to marry will not put up with any tricks. He has already made it clear that what he expects in a wife is obedience and hard work."

A quickly suppressed giggle came from one of the seats behind. Mr. Dubonnet turned and glared. Then, brushing an invisible fleck of dust from his sleeve, he returned his attention to Lizzie. "I should add that you will be his second wife. He is a widower." For a moment longer he held Lizzie's glance, then leisurely turned away.

The warning had been unmistakable. Lizzie was too shaken to move.

"Come on," Sarah urged, catching Lizzie's arm and pulling her to her feet. The crowd of men had only been waiting for Mr. Dubonnet to move away to close around them. Already they were surrounded. Forcing a path through the milling figures, Sarah hurried Lizzie out of the hall and back to their sleeping quarters.

For the first few moments after they sank down on their cots in the deserted barrack room, Lizzie was silent and trembling. But gradually the shivers lessened. "You know wot's worst of all?" she said in a small voice. "'Avin' everybody still think I'm guilty. Why cudn't 'e 'ave told them I didn't steal nothin'?"

Sarah didn't answer, for there was nothing she could say.

"D'you think yer 'usband will be as bad as mine?" Lizzie said after a moment. "D'you think they both just want somebody to work for 'em?"

"Probably."

"I wonder why yours don't want to be seen."

Again Sarah didn't answer. She couldn't admit even to Lizzie what she was fearing — that the man Mr. Dubonnet had picked out for her didn't want to show himself because he was too ugly — or because he was too old.

Chapter 21

By mid morning, more than half the girls had been spoken for. Some had accepted offers from miners who were panning nearby creeks. Others would be going as far north as Barkerville, Richfield and Camerontown.

"Too bad you two have to miss all the fun," Arabella announced smugly when she came flouncing down. "Four different men *all* want to marry me." She giggled. Sarah wondered if it had been her giggle they'd heard that morning. "I'm going to choose the richest." One more smug sideways glance at Lizzie, and Arabella disappeared back up the stairs.

Just before noon Mary Whitehead appeared in the sleeping quarters. Her face was flushed and her eyes were gleaming. "I think I've got a job!" she whispered, stopping beside Sarah.

"A job! But Mr. Dubonnet said there were no jobs for any of the governesses."

"Shhh!" In an excited undertone, Mary explained that one of the church committee ladies had sent a man over to speak to her. He didn't want a bride, but a nanny — someone to travel on the stage to Barkerville with him and his wife and help look after their children.

"'Ow many children?" Lizzie asked, moving closer.

"Five."

"Five!"

Mary smiled. "It's all right. I had four to look after in my last job in England."

"Any of these still babies?"

"Two."

"Cor!" Lizzie breathed.

"But you're not allowed to be a nanny," Sarah protested. "Mr. Dubonnet said he was going to make you be a bride."

Mary's voice dropped even lower. "That's why I can't let him find out. Mr. Peet says the stage leaves early tomorrow morning, and he's promised to come back sometime this afternoon and arrange exactly when and where I'm to meet them."

"You'll 'ave to sneak out!" Lizzie's eyes were dancing.

Mary nodded. "I'm going to collect my things now while no one else is here." Turning to her own bunk she tucked her belongings into her bag. It didn't take long. She looked around to make sure she hadn't forgotten anything, then set the bag down. "Now I'd better go back upstairs before Mr. Dubonnet notices I've gone and gets suspicious."

"Wot if one o' them other miners tries to claim you?" Lizzie warned.

A wry smile pulled at Mary's lips. Briefly her hand moved to her cheek and touched the glaring red birthmark. "There's not much chance of that till all the others are taken, and by then I'll be gone." Next moment, she'd disappeared back up the stairs.

"I wish we wos 'er," Lizzie said wistfully, watching her go. "Even with all them babies."

So did Sarah. If only she'd listened to Maud when her cousin said that this journey would end in disaster.

All afternoon a succession of girls came down to claim their belongings before going off to be married to their new husbands. Most looked nervous and apprehensive. When Fanny appeared, Sarah was surprised. Fanny's cheeks were flushed pink and her eyes were shining.

"Have you accepted someone too?" Sarah asked in wonder.

Fanny nodded. "He's only eighteen, but he says he's hard w–w–working. He'd walked m–m–most of the night to get here before we were all s–s–spoken for." The pink in Fanny's cheeks deepened to scarlet. "I showed him this." Shyly she opened her hand. In the palm lay the brooch Sarah had returned to her. "He promised to buy me a dress to w–w–wear it on."

"Cor," Lizzie breathed.

"He said he w–w–wished he'd had a chance to meet me mum." Brushing one hand quickly across her eyes, Fanny turned away.

Sarah couldn't answer for she didn't trust her voice. At least things had turned out well for Fanny.

It was almost suppertime when Mary returned. Even before she was close enough to speak, Sarah knew something was wrong.

"The church committee lady misunderstood," Mary confided in a tight voice. "They can't —" Her voice went funny. She coughed to clear it and started again. "They can't afford to hire a nanny after all. They're just offering to pay the stage fare for someone to travel with them to Barkerville and look after the children on the way."

"But they wouldn't just abandon you once you got there!" Sarah protested. "Surely they'd let you stay on for a little while, till you can find something else."

"What if I can't find something else?" Mary's hand crept to her cheek. "Sometimes I'm not very good at meeting strangers."

"Go anyways," Lizzie retorted.

The glimmer of a smile appeared on Mary's pale face. "At first I was going to. I decided I'd go even without a job. But I can't. Not when I've no friends there and no money. It's better to stay here."

Sarah's heart caught at the pain in Mary's voice. "Did you tell the man that?"

"Not yet. I asked if I could have a few minutes to think about it. But I'm going up now to tell him." As she spoke, Mary started toward the stairs.

"Mary, 'old on!" Lizzie moved toward her. "If you really 'n truly don't want to go," her voice dropped to an undertone, "'ow be me 'n Sarah go in your place?"

"No!" Sarah protested, but the word lacked conviction. If only they *could* take Mary's place. Next second, however, common sense returned. They couldn't go up to the gold fields without jobs any more than Mary could, for they, too, had no money and no friends.

"At least if we went we'd be able to stay together," Lizzie pointed out. "An' we wudn't be married off to 'usbands wot want to kill us with 'ard work."

"We'd be caught before we'd gone ten miles."

Lizzie's eyes were gleaming. "Not if we wos on a stage wif a family, looking after all them kids."

"Even if we weren't caught, we could starve or freeze to death during the winter. Barkerville is way up north. Besides," Sarah went on in an attempt to convince herself as well as Lizzie, "they only want one nanny."

"'Ow d'you know we aren't the only nannies they can get? Wot if everybody else is like Mary and won't go 'cos there's no pay an' no job once you get there?"

"That could be true," Mary agreed slowly. "They might not be able to get anyone else in time to leave tomorrow morning. They might be willing to take both of you. Shall I go upstairs and ask?"

"Yes!" Lizzie shouted.

Mary was watching Sarah.

She had found a spot on her skirt that seemed to need attention. She told herself to be sensible. She silently repeated all the arguments she'd just used — that it was craziness to think they could avoid being caught. And if by some stroke of luck they managed to get to Barkerville, they'd be no better off, for they'd starve or die of exposure before winter was over.

But the spark of excitement Lizzie's words had ignited refused to go out. At least this way they would have a chance, a voice suggested deep inside, and they might *not* starve or die of exposure. Besides, whatever happened couldn't be worse than the future Mr. Dubonnet had planned for them.

She could feel Mary's eyes watching her. At last she looked up. She nodded.

Lizzie beamed excitedly.

A few minutes later Mary was back with the news that if they wanted to go, they were to be at the stagecoach office at seven in the morning. "But Mr. Peet said I was to be sure to explain once again that they can't pay any wages. Like everyone else, he's going to Barkerville to try to find gold. He says he'll cover your stagecoach fare, and they'll let you live with them for a few days after you get there until you get settled, but that's all they can manage."

Lizzie continued to beam. "We kin find 'alf a dozen jobs in a few days."

"What if you can't?" Mary cautioned. "Maybe it's too risky."

"No riskier than 'avin' to go off wif them 'usbands wot Dubonnet 'as picked out for us," Lizzie retorted.

Sarah's heart was racing. She was remembering an evening on the *Tynemouth* when she sat beside her cousin's bunk. *"I'm glad we came, Saree,"* Maud had said. *"I have a feeling the chance is going to come for the exciting adventure you've dreamed about, and when it does, you must take it."*

Chapter 22

That night at bedtime Sarah went to Mary's bunk to say goodbye. "Will you be all right?" she asked shyly.

"Of course. That church committee lady may know of someone else who wants a nanny. If not, I'll be a bride." The words were cheerful, but Sarah knew the cheerfulness was forced. "Once all the other girls have been taken," Mary went on, one hand unconsciously lifting to the blemish on her cheek, "there's sure to be someone who won't worry too much about looks. Besides," a shy smile crept into her eyes, "if it's someone nice he might let me send for my sister." She pressed Sarah's hand. "But I'm worried about you two. Look after Lizzie. Don't let her do anything foolish."

For a moment Sarah clung to the hand that

had taken hold of hers. She wanted to tell Mary how frightened she was — that she didn't want to leave the other girls after all these weeks together — that she was terrified at the thought of going off into wild, unsettled country without any job or any money or any friends . . .

But Mary guessed without being told. "You'll be fine," she said quietly, once again pressing Sarah's hand. "As Lizzie pointed out, at least this way the two of you can stay together."

Somehow, knowing Mary understood made Sarah feel better.

She knew she should return to her own cot, for if they were to slip away unnoticed in the morning they had to be up early. But she was too keyed-up to sleep. Instead, she went to the window and gazed out. For the first time, she noticed the night sky brilliant with stars. Quickly she brushed at her eyes.

"Wot's wrong?" Lizzie said, moving up beside her.

For a moment Sarah didn't answer. She was too busy trying to swallow her unshed tears at the sight of the star-filled sky. Then she said softly, "Let's count them."

"Wot?"

"The stars." It was something she and Maud used to do. "You count on your side and I'll count on mine. After every hundred you get to make a wish."

Lizzie set to work eagerly. But Sarah had noticed one particularly bright star in her half of sky — the sort of star Maud always used as her starting point when they had counted stars together. Could Maud see it too? she wondered. Did people up there still wish on stars? Might Maud be wishing at this very moment — wishing for Sarah's sake that tomorrow might be the chance they'd talked about?

That thought brought such a rush of tears to Sarah's eyes that it was impossible to see the stars clearly enough to count any of them.

"Two hundred an' thirty–seven," Lizzie announced triumphantly. "I get two wishes." Closing her eyes tight, she concentrated hard. "You want to 'ear wot I wished for?"

"No. If you tell a wish it won't come true," Sarah managed through lips that threatened to tremble. She turned away. "If we're going to slip out early in the morning, we'd better go to bed."

It was impossible to fall asleep. Sarah's mind churned with questions. What if they over-slept? If they were late Mr. Peet and his family would go without them. What if they couldn't find the stagecoach office? "Near the water," was all Mary knew. "Watch for some sign of a ferry," she'd said. Worst of all, what if they were caught? What extra punishment would Mr. Dubonnet find for them?

The first fear proved groundless. Far from oversleeping, Sarah hardly slept at all. Shortly after five she wakened Lizzie. Listening for any sound that might suggest one of the other girls was stirring, they dressed silently in the dark then crept to the door. The bolt slipped back effortlessly. Next moment they were outside, clutching their few belongings in the well-worn carpetbags. Then Sarah stopped in dismay, for it was pouring rain and bitingly cold. She wanted to run back inside. Perhaps this was an omen — proof that they should give up this crazy idea — that it would only end in disaster . . .

"Rain's wot brings luck, didn't you know?" Lizzie said brightly, swinging her carpetbag and starting off down the street.

At Lizzie's words, Sarah's panic faded, just as it had that first moment below decks on the *Tynemouth*. She moved after Lizzie.

But her fear of being caught grew stronger with every step. She kept glancing back over her shoulder. By now, the pushed-back bolt on the Marine Barracks door was sure to have been discovered. Word of their disappearance was probably already on its way to Mr. Dubonnet or Mrs. Worthing. Mr. Dubonnet would immediately guess where they'd gone. Right this minute he'd be sending someone after them —

"'Ere we are!" Lizzie announced brightly, entering the door of the stagecoach office half-buried among a group of other buildings.

Wet through and shivering with cold, Sarah hurried after her. Mr. Peet and his family were waiting. Fifteen minutes later the entire group boarded the ferry, and the ferry took off.

Miraculously, Sarah's spirits lifted. Perhaps they hadn't been followed after all! She glanced around. A brisk wind was churning the ocean water into choppy waves. It reminded her of the *Tynemouth*, and for a moment she worried about seasickness. But standing in the fresh air on an open ferry was different from being shut below decks, she discovered. No one was sick and everyone enjoyed themselves — particularly the children, for they had room to play.

"Which they won't have once we board the stagecoach," Mrs. Peet admitted with a wry smile. "That's why I wanted you two girls to travel with us."

The square–closed coach was waiting when the ferry docked. It was hitched to two pairs of high-spirited black horses, with the driver sitting behind them on a high box seat. His hands held a double set of reins, and his feet were braced against a foot rail in case any heavy pulling might be required.

The coach held two bench seats inside for passengers, one facing forward, the other back, and a third bench seat outside on the roof. The children begged to sit there, but to Sarah and Mrs. Peet's relief, the driver said only adults could ride on top.

The last piece of baggage was strapped to the back of the coach, all the passengers were told to get on board, and the driver whipped up his team.

For the first few miles, the excitement of riding by stage held the children silent and fascinated. Then the novelty wore off. Before the first day was over, Sarah understood why Mrs. Peet had been eager to have them travel with her. Even two nannies weren't enough. They could have used five. How did one amuse a small child from dawn until dark on a rocking, swaying coach where there was no room to move around or even to change position? But though each day of the journey seemed more tedious to the children, it was one day closer to freedom for Sarah and Lizzie.

At Yale they changed to the Barnard Express stagecoach which would take them the rest of the way to Barkerville. Sarah and Mrs. Peet found the change a nuisance, but Lizzie was bubbling. "Now we'll be even 'arder to trace," she said.

Until that moment, it hadn't occurred to Sarah that Lizzie was happier and more carefree than she'd been in weeks. With a shock she realized the reason — *"Why couldn't 'e 'ave told people I didn't steal nothin,"* Lizzie had said that first morning at the Marine Barracks. Instead, Dubonnet had kept subtly reminding everyone that Lizzie was a thief — the passengers on the *Tynemouth*, the crew, even the church committee ladies who met them in Victoria. No wonder she had been crushed by that blanket of distrust and suspicion. Now at last she was out from under it.

At least she was out from under it as long as Mr. Dubonnet didn't guess where they'd gone and start spreading rumors about Lizzie up in Barkerville, Sarah reminded herself. That was exactly the sort of thing he might do, and for a moment she wondered if she should warn Lizzie to be on her guard. But she pushed away her worry. How could Mr. Dubonnet spread rumors about Lizzie in Barkerville when he was hundreds of miles away in Victoria?

Chapter 23

Late in the afternoon on their eleventh day of traveling, the Barnard Express stage pulled into Barkerville.

Sarah's first impression was of a toy town made for a children's playroom. All the buildings sat up off the ground on wooden stilts, and all were connected by raised wooden sidewalks. She was just about to ask why when the stagecoach driver provided the answer.

"Because of the mud," he explained. "Every spring when the run–off comes this whole area is four or five feet deep in gumbo. You can lose your boots before you've taken two steps. Then in the winter there's up to eight feet of snow. Without raised walkways, we couldn't get around anywhere."

"Eight feet of snow!" Sarah exclaimed under

her breath to Lizzie. "And we only have shawls and flat orphanage boots!"

"It ain't winter yet," Lizzie said irrepressibly. "By then we'll 'ave found a way to buy lots of warm clothes."

Mr. Peet asked directions to the cabin he'd arranged to rent for the winter. It belonged to a friend who had decided to wait till spring to continue his own search for gold. It was a short distance out of Barkerville on the road leading to the cemetery, and to everyone's relief it turned out to be much larger than most of the other cabins. It had a large main room that served as a sitting room, kitchen and eating area, two tiny bedrooms along the rear wall created by the addition of a wood partition, and at the top of a ladder on the back wall, a small wooden platform under the roof making another sleeping area. This was the space Mrs. Peet said Sarah and Lizzie could use for the next few days.

They helped her unpack and settle the children, then with the promise to be back later, set off to explore.

"An' find a job," Lizzie added.

A walk down one side of the main street then back up the other brought them half a dozen grinning offers of marriage, twice that many requests for a kiss, but no possibilities for work. However, when they reached the bottom of the street, they discovered that the town had a second street in behind. This one had no showy buildings up on stilts and no connecting wooden walkways. Its buildings sat right down in the gumbo, and included a clutter of barren, unpainted prospectors' shacks, several residences housing the town's Chinese population, three stables, a bakery, and a laundry.

"That's wot we kin do!" Lizzie said excitedly. "I know all about doin' wash. Matron made me work in the orphanage laundry the 'ole time I wos there. Come on!" Without waiting, she crossed the street and pushed through the door of the small, humid shop.

Two silent Chinese faces stared back at her.

It was ten minutes before Sarah could convince Lizzie that the proprietors were trying, in their own language, to tell her that it didn't matter whether she had lots of laundry experience or not, they weren't interested in hiring any helpers.

"Then we'll start a laundry of our own," Lizzie said brightly, coming back out into the sunshine.

"How?"

"Somethin' will turn up."

But despite Lizzie's cheery pose, even she was discouraged as the walk continued. Instead of the rich gold town they had expected, they were seeing desperate poverty. Compared with the cabin Mr. Peet had procured, these miners' shacks were tiny and barren, put together of roughly-hewn boards with no caulking between them. The raw wind blew easily through the wide cracks, and there were no glass panes in any of the window openings. If they were blocked at all it was with newspaper, but most stood open to the air.

"If it's forty below 'ere in the winter like wot that stage driver told us, 'ow can anybody live?" Lizzie said in awe, staring at the ill-made cabins.

It seemed few of the cabin owners bothered to close their doors when they went off in the morning to pan the creeks. As Sarah and Lizzie continued down the dreary street they could see right into most of the buildings.

They were as barren inside as out. All had wooden bunks, some with blankets on them, but none with mattresses. A few cabins boasted a metal stove, but most had just a circle of rocks on the earth floor where a fire could be laid. Some had a wooden bench or a straight-backed chair for sitting on, but many more had only boxes or packing crates. And any rough, homemade dish cupboards hammered to the wall held nothing but a few unmatched plates, tin cups and blackened cooking pots.

Sarah was so discouraged she was just about to say they should turn back, when Lizzie stopped in front of one of the cabins. "Did you 'ear somebody groanin'?" Without waiting for an answer she walked up to the door and pushed it open.

"Lizzie! You can't just barge in!"

"'Oo's bargin' in? I think somebody's sick." As if that explained everything, Lizzie disappeared inside.

Hesitantly, Sarah followed.

The cabin, like so many of the others they'd

passed, had two wooden bunks nailed to the wall and a single wooden chair in front of the unpaned window. But unlike many of the others, this one had a metal stove. It also had a large, square washtub leaning against the back wall. And in the customary homemade cupboard half a dozen leather-bound books sat next to the unmatched dishes.

Then Sarah noticed how cold and damp it felt inside the small building, and the funny smell. It made her throat want to close. Where could it be coming from?

Lizzie had gone straight to one of the bunks and was bending over it. With a start, Sarah realized someone was lying there. His eyes were closed, and he was lying so still under a grimy grey blanket that until that moment she hadn't noticed him.

"I'm goin' to build up the fire," Lizzie announced, moving back from the bunk. Closing the door, she reached for a piece of wood from the box beside the stove.

With the door closed, the smell grew even more unpleasant. Again Sarah looked around, but she couldn't see anything that might account for it.

As the warmth from the fire began to fill the cottage the figure on the bed stirred. He opened his eyes.

"Kin we 'elp?" Lizzie asked looking down at him.

For a moment the man on the bunk looked surprised. Then, as if it was too much trouble to worry about where two strange girls had appeared from, his expression changed to a welcoming smile. "Would you —" His voice was faint. He coughed to clear it and said again more firmly, "Would you make me some tea?"

Relieved that the man didn't seem to mind their barging in uninvited, Sarah went to help. There was a kettle on top of the stove and a pail of water in the corner, but it was several minutes before they discovered the tea in a tin box at the back of the cupboard.

They finally succeeded in getting the water to boil, then steeped the tea till it was black and strong. Lizzie was just pouring a cup when the door of the shack was pushed open. A tall bearded figure stood in the doorway. His initial surprise at the sight of the girls changed to worry. "Is something wrong? Is Charlie worse?" Without waiting for an answer he started toward the bed. But far from being worse, the man on the bunk was grinning.

The newcomer stopped. He turned around. "Who are you?" he demanded of Lizzie.

She put the mug of hot tea she was holding into the sick man's hands, waited to make sure he could manage, then said matter-of-factly, "We come on the stage. I'm Lizzie and she's Sarah. 'Oo are you?"

The humor of the situation must have hit the newcomer for he started to laugh. "We came on the stage, too — only we came a year ago. I'm Bill and he's Charlie." He nodded toward the man in the bunk.

"To 'unt fer gold?" Lizzie asked eagerly. "'Ave you found some?"

"Not yet." Bill's smile broadened. "But what would be the fun of adventuring if it was too easy?"

Sarah had been edging closer to the door, intending to tell Lizzie they had to leave, but at Bill's words she stopped and looked at him with new interest.

Lizzie's attention had returned to the figure in the bunk. "So, why's 'e sick?"

"He's got gumboot fever."

"Gum wot?"

"Gumboot fever." Bill moved closer to the bed and gently lifted the blanket off the sick man's legs. From just below the knee right down to the toes they were wrapped in yellow stained bandages. "It's from standing day after day in the icy cold creek water."

"Why wud 'e do that?" Lizzie's voice was disbelieving.

For a second, amusement registered in Bill's dark eyes, then his voice turned dry. "During the last little while, we've both been asking ourselves the same question. Unfortunately, that's where a lot of the gold is — on the rocky bottom of the creek beds."

Sarah was staring at Charlie. That's where the smell was coming from, she realized with a shock. Infection. All at once she remembered something else the stage driver had told them this morning, together with the explanation about the mud and the snow and the wooden sidewalks. He'd pointed out the cemetery on the side of the hill and a dozen newly filled-in graves. "Gumboot fever," he'd said shortly.

"Can't you do something?" she asked.

"Umm–hmmm, and we will," Bill answered calmly. "Just as soon as we make our strike we're climbing on the stage and getting out of here."

"Why don't you go now," Sarah suggested, "then come back after he's well?"

"No!" This time it was Charlie who spoke. His voice was surprisingly firm and determined. "Not till we make our strike." He turned to Bill. "You promised we'd stay till then, Bill. You can't go back on your word now!"

"I won't go back on it, Charlie," Bill said quietly. But Sarah saw the worry in his eyes.

"People find gold all the time," Charlie rushed on. "Any day now it will be our turn. Right?"

Again Bill nodded. Then his expression softened into a wry smile. "Besides, even if we wanted to leave we couldn't. You're hardly in shape to walk out and we haven't money for the stage."

"We wouldn't leave even if we did," Charlie insisted. A faraway look came into his eyes and for the first time he smiled. "We're staying till we make our strike — then we're going to buy that land."

For a moment after that neither man said anything.

Sarah moved forward and took the empty cup from Charlie's hand. "We'd better go," she told

Lizzie. Rinsing the cup with water, she returned it to the wooden cupboard and moved toward the door.

"Can't you stay for a while longer? Or could you come tomorrow?" Bill said. Then, as if he was afraid she was going to refuse, he added, "For Charlie's sake?" His face softened. "It's dreary here by himself all day — particularly when he's not feeling well."

"'Course we'll come," Lizzie said brightly.

Sarah glanced over at her. Surely Lizzie must realize they couldn't start nursing sick miners no matter how sorry they felt for them. They had to find jobs so they could support themselves. Still, maybe it wouldn't hurt to come for a day or two. "We could probably come tomorrow for a little while and check on Charlie," she agreed.

"Will you stay till I get home in case I need checking on too?"

Quickly, Sarah looked up, for an odd note had come into Bill's voice. Was he serious or teasing? She couldn't be sure. But there was no way to find out, for already he was chatting to Charlie about something else, as if he didn't even remember he'd asked a question.

Next day as promised they went to check on Charlie. They tidied the cabin, kept the stove going and made him tea.

"Wot d'you think?" Lizzie said when they'd finished. "Should we go 'ome now, in case Mrs. Peet needs us?"

All afternoon Sarah had been telling herself

she had no intention of staying once their chores were finished, but now that it was time to go she realized she didn't want to. All day she'd been remembering what Bill had said about adventuring being no fun if it was too easy. She wanted to talk to him again — to ask him to explain.

"I suppose we really should stay till Bill gets home," she said in an offhand tone, concentrating on some dirt on the toe of her heavy orphanage boot. "After all, we did sort of promise."

"Yes, please stay," Charlie urged.

Ever since the daylight had started to fade, Charlie's excitement had been building. Now, in a voice tight with eagerness he confided, "This is the day Bill's going to make our strike. I have a feeling about it." His eyes were focused on the closed door.

As steps sounded on the path outside Sarah found herself watching the door as well.

Next moment Bill pushed it open. He paused in the doorway, looked over at Charlie, smiled whimsically and shook his head.

For a second, disappointment flooded Charlie's pale face, but almost immediately it was gone. "Tomorrow. It'll be tomorrow, Bill. All day I've had this hunch inside."

Bill nodded. He closed the door, then turned to Sarah and Lizzie. His face brightened.

He seemed so happy to see them that Sarah was glad they'd stayed.

She listened fascinated as he recounted story

after story about their adventures in the gold fields, and about why he and Charlie had come.

"As soon as we've made our strike we're going back to England to buy this piece of land," he said, a dreamy note creeping into his voice. "We knew it was the place we wanted the minute we saw it. It's got trees thick with birds, and rolling fields, and a meadow with a stream running through."

Charlie was staring into the middle distance as if he were already there.

"We've put in an offer for it, and they've agreed to hold it for us," Bill went on. "Now all we need is the money."

"Is it fer a farm?" Lizzie asked.

"A horse farm." It was Charlie who answered this time. He was still concentrating on something just out of sight. "Like the one we used to own. As soon as we make our strike we're going home to buy it."

"You two owned an 'orse farm?" Lizzie asked in wonder.

"Not Bill, just me. My father owned it and I grew up there." Charlie's voice tightened. "My family would still own it if I —" He broke off abruptly, then in a completely different tone said, "Bill and I are going to start a new one."

Sarah waited for him to go on — to explain — but instead Bill said brightly, "That's enough about us. Tell us about you. Why did you come here?"

To Sarah's surprise, she found herself telling him things she'd never intended to tell anyone —

about the *Tynemouth*, and Maud, and how she'd been sure this was going to be her chance to make something of her life.

The smile in Bill's eyes deepened. "The adventure you'd been waiting for," he said softly.

Sarah's startled gaze flew to his face. "How did you —"

"*The day shall not be up so soon as I, To try the fair adventure of tomorrow*," he quoted softly.

Sarah's surprise changed to delight. "I remember that! It's from *King John*! Uncle Tor used to read us all of Shakespeare's plays!" She caught the glimmer of surprised approval that crossed Bill's face, but next moment it was forgotten as a wave of loneliness swept over her for Maud and home and Uncle Tor. Swallowing hard she pushed the loneliness away. "Instead of this being the adventure I'd hoped for," she admitted in a low, unsteady voice, "we discovered we were being sent to the gold fields to be brides for the miners. They considered us no different from common street girls —"

She broke off in confusion. If only she could call the words back. What if now he, too, thought she was a street girl? She didn't understand why she should care for his good opinion. She hardly knew him — but for some reason she couldn't bear to have him and Charlie start ogling them and making jokes. She looked away and braced herself for what was sure to come.

Instead Bill said quietly, "I'm glad you didn't let that happen. I'm glad you came up here instead." His voice had softened in a way that gave her a funny feeling inside. Crossing the floor to the wooden shelf on the back wall, he took down one of the leather-bound books. "Take this home with you for a few days." It was a collection of Shakespeare's plays.

Such a wave of conflicting emotions swept over Sarah that she was thrown off balance. She managed something she hoped would pass for thanks, accepted the book without even glancing up, and moved toward the door. Next moment, she was safely out in the evening shadows.

To her relief, Lizzie followed without argument.

All the way home, she berated herself for having talked so frankly. True, Bill hadn't made any jokes, but that didn't mean he wouldn't betray her confidence to the other men when he was out in the creek beds. They would think it was a great joke.

But even that couldn't destroy her pleasure in the book he had loaned her. She tucked it under her blanket, then next morning, as soon as it was light, long before Mrs. Peet or any of the children were awake, she took it out and began to read.

Reluctantly, when the first sounds of stirring came from below, she tucked it away again.

She was still thinking of Bill as she and Lizzie walked the mile and a half to the small prospectors' cabin. Sooner or later she knew they had to find jobs to support themselves.

But they could postpone that for a little while, she rationalized. They could come and look after Charlie and Bill for a few more days, surely . . .

But next morning Mrs. Peet took her aside. "I'm afraid we can't afford to keep you and Lizzie any longer," she said with regret. "Mr. Peet says he doesn't know how we'll make it through the winter as it is. After tomorrow, we'll have to ask you girls to go off on your own."

For the first time Sarah admitted to herself how much Bill's friendship meant to her.

All morning, while they were together at the cabin she avoided telling Lizzie. But after lunch when Charlie was napping she knew she couldn't put it off any longer.

"Why didn't you tell me sooner?" Lizzie accused.

"I didn't want to spoil things."

Lizzie glanced toward the man on the bed. Charlie's fever had grown worse. He never seemed to stop shivering now, not even when the fire was going. "'Ow kin we stop comin' when 'e needs us?"

"I know. But if we can't stay on with Mrs. Peet then we've got to find jobs." Mixed with her sharp disappointment Sarah could hear the fear in her own voice. She was remembering what Mary had said about no job and no money and no friends.

"We can't turn our backs on Charlie," Lizzie said stubbornly.

It was true. "But what else can we do?"

"'Ope somethin' turns up. Mebbe Bill'll come 'ome tonight and tells us 'e's made that strike, so's we kin ask 'im to lend us somethin'.'"

Sarah was about to tell Lizzie to be serious when she realized her friend was struggling to hide her own terror.

Again, as the afternoon drew to a close Charlie began watching the door. Again Bill came in with no good news.

"Tomorrow," Charlie said as before.

Sarah knew if she didn't tell them right away she wouldn't tell them at all. So in the moment's silence following Charlie's remark, she announced bluntly, "We can't come any more."

Both Bill and Charlie stared at her in disbelief.

"It's not that we don't want to," she went on quickly, "but we've got to find work." She told them what Mrs. Peet had said that morning.

"But I thought we were all —" Whatever Bill had started to say, he must have thought better of, for he broke off. Then in a tone Sarah had never heard before he continued, "Fine. Thanks for coming for a couple of days, at least." He turned away.

Lizzie was staring at the large, square washtub propped against the back wall of the cabin. "Mebbe if you'd give us the use of that," she said thoughtfully, spacing out the words, "we cud keep comin' after all."

"Stop making everything a joke," Sarah snapped, more upset than she wanted to admit.

"'Oo's jokin'?" Ignoring Sarah, Lizzie turned to Bill. "Kin we use that tub?"

"What? Oh — I suppose so." His tone made it clear his thoughts were on something else.

Lizzie's face broke into a grin. "I knew somethin' wud turn up! If we kin use that tub then we don't 'ave to look fer other jobs. We kin look after Charlie an' earn money at the same time — doin' washin' fer people." She turned to Sarah. "Don't you see? With wot we earn we kin pay Mrs. Peet fer keepin' us. An' if we kin pay 'er, I bet she'll let us stay on there as long as we want. All right?"

The numb emptiness in Sarah's middle miraculously disappeared. Quickly she glanced over at Bill, then looked away again even more quickly, afraid he would read more into her feelings than was there. She was determined not to depend on him or any man. She wasn't going to end up like Momma.

Adventurers had to be independent. Bill of all people should understand that, she reassured herself, for he was an adventurer too.

Chapter 24

That evening they told Mrs. Peet what they planned. She agreed they could stay with her for one or two more days while they tried to get a laundry business going.

Next morning, while Lizzie went to the cabin to care for Charlie, Sarah visited every business in Barkerville. At first no one was interested, until she announced that she and Lizzie would do laundry at half what the Chinese laundry was charging. Then work poured in. Several people gave her laundry to do that very day, and others told her to call back the following morning.

It wasn't the sort of job she'd been dreaming of, but it meant they could support themselves and still look after Charlie.

She hurried back to the cabin with the washing to tell Lizzie and Charlie the good news. When Bill came home, they told him too. Then, promising to be back early the next morning, she and Lizzie returned to Mrs. Peet's cabin with their first day's earnings.

"Tomorrow will be even better," Sarah told her.

It was.

By the third day business was so good Lizzie suggested moving the washtub outside where the noise and commotion wouldn't disturb Charlie. "Then we kin take turns," she added. "One kin stay outside washin', rinsin' and wringin', while the other stays in and keeps watch." For, despite their efforts, each day Charlie seemed to grow weaker.

In the afternoons when it was her turn to sit with Charlie, Sarah read to him from one of the books on their bookshelf. She'd brought back the collection of Shakespeare and often she read from that, but Charlie's favorite was Plutarch's *Lives*. Often when Bill arrived home, she and Charlie were still deep in discussion about what they'd read, and Bill enthusiastically joined in.

One day, under the folds of her shawl, Sarah brought Maud's book of poems to the cabin. She wasn't sure Charlie liked poetry, but once she had started reading he begged her to go on. The poem he liked best was the one that had been Maud's favorite:

> *"You'll not be with me when the spring is here.*
> *But I'll remember other happier springs*
> *When distance did not part us . . . ."*

He smiled as he listened, then asked her to tell him about her cousin Maud.

"She was heartbroken when her book was stolen," Sarah said as she finished recounting what had happened. "It seemed such a cruel thing for Mr. Dubonnet to have done. Why would he steal it? He wasn't the sort of man to even like poetry, and he must have known there was little chance of being able to sell such a book. Anyone on board with money to spare would have used it for food or medicine, not poetry."

"Perhaps he thought pretending to be a poetry lover would make him look well-educated," Charlie suggested. He grinned. "He might even have been intending to memorize some of the poems and pass them off as his own."

There was silence for a moment, then Charlie asked quietly if she would read that same poem again.

Just as she started, the door opened behind her. Assuming it was Bill, she kept reading. By the time she finished Charlie had drifted off to sleep.

"That's beautiful. Will you read another one?" a quiet voice said from the doorway.

Startled, Sarah swung around. It wasn't Bill after all, but a perfect stranger. Embarrassed, Sarah closed the book and got to her feet, for the man who was studying her so intently didn't look friendly and easy going like Bill or Charlie. He looked businesslike and successful. He was wearing polished shoes instead of thick-soled boots, a neat suit in place of coarse work pants, and a shirt with a fancy collar.

"Don't be alarmed," the newcomer said reassuringly, keeping his voice low so it wouldn't disturb Charlie. "Mrs. Peet sent me 'round to speak to you." He smiled. "She knows of my ambitions to start a library here some day, and thought we should meet." He nodded toward the book Sarah was still holding. "All too few girls are ever given the opportunity to learn to read."

Sarah's mind filled with memories of the hours she and Maud and Uncle Tor had spent pouring over his books. It was in her uncle's library that she'd learned to accept Momma's death. "I was lucky," she admitted softly. "My uncle taught me to love books."

The stranger seemed surprised. "But didn't you come on the *Tynemouth*? I thought all the *Tynemouth* girls were orphans."

Sarah's pleasure changed to numb horror. If he knew she'd come on the *Tynemouth*, Bill must have told him, for she hadn't confessed that to anyone else except Charlie. If Bill had told this stranger, then he'd probably told others too. Already word might have reached Mr. Dubonnet. He might be making plans right this minute to send someone to bring them back. But somehow that thought didn't seem as awful as knowing that Bill had broken faith with her — that he'd laughed and joked with the other men about her . . .

The man read her alarm. "It was Mrs. Peet

who mentioned you'd come with the *Tynemouth* girls," he said quickly. "But I haven't said a word to anyone else and I won't if you would prefer that I didn't."

The wave of relief that washed over Sarah was so strong she put her hand on the back of the chair to steady herself. Bill hadn't broken faith with her after all.

"Tell me about the poem you were reading," the stranger continued.

Relieved to change the direction of her thoughts, Sarah explained about Maud and Harley.

"Your cousin would have fitted right in here," the visitor said softly when she finished. "As I'm sure you've discovered, the men who've come here to prospect for gold are some of the best educated and best read people I have ever met." He smiled wryly. "Though they might have been wiser to use the space in their packs for warm clothes and cooking pots instead of books."

In spite of herself, Sarah smiled, for that was certainly true of Bill and Charlie.

"The reason Mrs. Peet sent me 'round to speak to you is because she knows of my library plans and recommends you highly as a possible librarian."

A librarian! For a moment Sarah was too stunned to speak.

"As I say, my Barkerville library won't be built for several years yet. First I have to get the money to finance it. But meantime I have a friend in Victoria who runs the library there.

Should you want a job, just let me know and I'll write to him."

For almost ten minutes after the stranger left, Sarah sat staring into space, daydreaming. Then she came down to earth.

"'Oo wos that?" Lizzie asked, coming in from rinsing some shirts.

"He said his name was John Bowron." She repeated what he'd said about speaking to his friend at the Victoria library about getting her a job.

"Cor!" Lizzie breathed in wonder. "Wudn't that be somethin'?"

Sarah nodded. Then she firmly pushed away the daydream. "It would be something, if I could take it. But of course I can't."

"Cos it's in Victoria?"

Sarah nodded. "If I went back there, how long do you think it would take Mr. Dubonnet to realize who I was?"

Chapter 25

Several days later, Mrs. Peet came home from the Barnard Express office with the news that a young Anglican missionary was expected to arrive in the gold town the following day.

"He must be more of a fool than most," Bill remarked that evening when Sarah passed on the information. He stirred the tea she'd fixed for him. "He should know that telling people ahead of time that he's coming is just an invitation to these miners."

"Invitation?" Sarah asked.

"To plan some trick. They don't like the missionaries coming up here talking gloom, doom and damnation."

"I wonder how long he plans to stay," Charlie said, his voice casual.

"Not long once the boys start hazing him."

"Wot's 'azing?" said Lizzie.

"Teasing, interrupting, maybe tossing a few rotten vegetables," Bill replied.

"If he —" Charlie cleared his throat and started again. "If he does come, I'd like to talk to him." He sounded self–conscious.

The laughter left Bill's face. He moved closer to the bunk. "Of course, if you like, Charlie. But you don't need a preacher. You're going to be fine."

Charlie was busy straightening the top of his blanket. "I know." His voice was even more casual. "Just the same, will you see if you can arrange it?"

All the next day Charlie scarcely allowed himself to doze. He lay wide awake, watching the door, waiting for the missionary to arrive. But there was no sign of him. That evening, when Bill came home, Charlie asked what had happened.

"I don't know," Bill told him, puzzled. "Nobody's seen him. He must've changed his mind and decided not to come after all."

"Maybe he'll come tomorrow. If he does, will you bring him around?"

Bill nodded. But there was no sign of the missionary that day either.

If Charlie was disappointed, he kept it to himself, and no one mentioned it again.

Each day now, it seemed the quantity of laundry was increasing. Sarah was delighted because it meant they could pay Mrs. Peet and still have some left over to put in their indepen-dence fund. But some days she worried about being able to get all the work done. This was one of those days. They'd seemed to be behind ever since the day started. So, after lunch, when Charlie was half asleep and as comfortable as they could make him, she and Lizzie went outside to work on the laundry together.

"Call if you need anything," Sarah told Charlie.

They were both elbow deep in soapy water when a tall, thin, disheveled-looking young man came down the road beside the row of cabins. At the sight of the laundry tub he paused, then moved closer.

"Would you . . . wash a shirt for me?" he asked in a soft, shy voice.

Sarah gazed in surprise, for he wasn't carrying any laundry.

But Lizzie grinned. "We kin wash yer shirt and yer pants, too, if you want." She nodded toward his soaking wet, mud-spattered clothes. "Wot 'appened?"

"I fell in the creek — at least I fell in after I was helped with a little push," he admitted with a shy smile.

Lizzie giggled. She nodded toward the cabin. "You kin go in there and wrap yerself in a blanket till things is dry."

"I'd better go in first and explain to Charlie," Sarah said, straightening up from the washtub and moving toward the cabin door.

"This 'ere's that missionary," Lizzie explained in a surprised voice when Sarah came back outside. "The one Mrs. Peet said wos comin'. 'E wos put onto the wrong road at Lightnin' Creek and got lost, which is why 'e's late." As an after thought she added, "'Is name is Josh."

The young man colored self-consciously. "Josh Gillmor. I guess I'm easy game when it comes to practical jokes. I don't seem to have much sense of direction."

"Is that 'ow you ended up in the creek, too?"

Again the slow, shy smile crept over his face. He shook his head. "That was because I turned my back when I shouldn't have."

Sarah burst out laughing.

"I told 'im about Charlie," Lizzie said.

Josh's face brightened. "I'm glad he wants to talk to me. You'd be surprised how few miners have time for religion." He moved several steps toward the cabin then turned back. "Did you say there was a blanket I could use?" Again his face flushed with embarrassment.

"Take the one off the second bunk," Sarah directed.

"An' we promise not to peek!" Lizzie told him mischievously.

Josh disappeared into the cabin. A moment later, his head and one bare arm appeared around the door long enough to hand out his muddy clothes.

In spite of the brisk wind that had come up, it was almost dark before Josh's clothes were dry enough to put back on, but neither he nor Charlie seemed to have noticed the time.

They were still talking quietly when Bill came home, tired and more discouraged than he wanted to let on. Forcing a smile, he set down the two round panning dishes he always took with him in case one got damaged and turned to shake hands with Josh.

"Will you come again tomorrow?" Charlie asked a few minutes later as Josh and Bill finished talking and Josh prepared to leave.

Josh promised he would.

Next day Charlie's fever had grown worse. Josh stayed with him all day and again they talked almost steadily. Sarah was delighted, for it meant she and Lizzie could work together on the backlog of laundry. Whenever Charlie fell asleep for a little while, Josh came out and offered to help as well.

Once, when Lizzie went back inside to build up the fire, Josh said quietly, "I envy you having Lizzie for a friend. I was telling her how lonely and discouraging it gets sometimes trying to be a missionary, particularly when you know you're not very clever and are a lot younger than most of the fellows you're supposed to be preaching to. D'you know what she said?" The familiar self-conscious smile crept over his face. "She said to stop worrying about all the things I wasn't, and to just go ahead and be myself."

At supper time on Wednesday evening Charlie seemed happier and more contented than Sarah had ever seen him.

Josh came again on both Thursday and Friday. The fever continued to worsen. Charlie was too tired now to talk at all, but he was happy to have Josh with him. Then sometime after lunch on Friday afternoon he fell into a deep sleep.

He didn't wake up.

"He asked me to promise I'd give him a proper funeral," Josh told Bill that evening.

Bill nodded.

"How old was he?"

"Twenty," Bill replied.

Not much older than Maud, Sarah realized. That night, for the first time in weeks, she took Penelope from her haven in the bottom of the carpetbag. For the dark places, Momma had said. As Sarah settled down to sleep she hugged the doll tightly in her arms.

"We'll find some place else to run our laundry business," she told Bill next morning as they returned to the cabin after the funeral. "Now that Charlie —"

"No! Please stay." His voice softened and he added, "It would make things easier for me."

"Fer us too," Lizzie put in before Sarah could answer. The twinkle crept back into her eyes. "'Oo else up 'ere 'as one of them big washtubs wot they'll lend us?"

Bill laughed, but lines of pain and loneliness troughed his face.

"I let Charlie down," he told Sarah a few minutes later, sounding as if he was speaking more to himself than to her. He was staring out the unpaned window toward the cemetery on the hillside. "Somehow I should have found a way to make that strike. He was counting on me."

Sarah didn't know what to say, so she kept silent.

"Then he could have made things right."

"How do you mean?"

For a moment Sarah thought Bill hadn't heard, or wasn't going to answer, for he continued to stare out the window. Then in a voice so low she had to strain to hear, he said, "Charlie was off adventuring in London when he heard his father was sick. He should have gone home and taken over, for he knew his mother couldn't run a horse farm, and his brothers were just little boys. But he kept putting it off." Bill's voice dropped even lower. "Looking after your family and a horse farm doesn't seem very glamorous or exciting when you're eighteen."

For a moment, Sarah thought he wasn't going to say anything more, then, rubbing the back of his hand across his mouth, he continued. "By the time he finally decided to go home and see if they were all right, the farm was so deep in debt it had to be sold."

"This new farm was for them?"

Bill nodded. "They were going to live there. Charlie was going to live there with them to run it, and I was going to be his business advisor." He turned away. Brushing a hand across his eyes, he added gruffly, "I'm going for a walk."

As Sarah watched him go, she found herself hoping he had something for *his* dark places. She wanted to ask, but she didn't know how.

But next second she told herself to stop being foolish. She had to stop worrying about him.

She had to stop even thinking about him. Now that Charlie was gone Bill wouldn't stay in the gold fields much longer. Any day now he'd pack up and leave, and when he did, he'd never think of her again. She wasn't going to be like Momma, spending her life waiting for someone who never gave her a thought.

Next morning, as Lizzie and Sarah were starting their washing, Josh came 'round to say he had to head back. He had services planned, he said, in Richfield, Lightning Creek, Lillooet and Clinton before returning to Victoria. At least, he added wryly, he did if the miners didn't shout him down or push him in the creek again. But first he wondered if Lizzie would go for a walk.

She came back beaming. "'E says 'e loves me," she confessed in a shy undertone. "'E says 'e wants to marry me."

Sarah wasn't surprised. Ever since the day Josh had talked privately to her about having Lizzie for a friend she'd suspected this might be coming. She finished rinsing the shirt she'd been working on and said carefully, "You've only known him a few days. Are you sure you like him well enough?"

Lizzie nodded shyly. Her cheeks reddened. "It's the first time in me 'ole life I've loved someone 'oo loves me back." Pushing up her sleeves, she joined Sarah at the washtub.

They worked in silence for a few minutes. Then Lizzie said thoughtfully, "Josh says we'll get married as soon as 'e gets the bishop's permission. Wot if this bishop says no?"

"He won't, Silly."

Lizzie gave the shirt she was working on a few more good scrubs, a happy glow in her eyes. "'Oo'd 'ave thought I'd end up marryin' a preacher?"

But after a few moments she stopped again. Her face clouded. "Wot about you? I can't take off an' leave you 'ere all on your own."

"I'm not on my own. I've Mrs. Peet to look after me. We've enough saved that I can buy a washtub of my own after Bill leaves and keep on with the laundry till something more exciting turns up. Who knows — Mr. Bowron might even know someone living somewhere besides Victoria who is looking for a librarian."

"Wudn't that be somethin'!" Reassured, Lizzie plunged her arms back into the depths of the soapy water. "Think wot we'd 'ave missed if we 'adn't foxed old Dubonnet and taken Mary's place."

Sarah nodded. So much had happened since that morning when they'd crept out of the Marine Barracks that she'd scarcely thought about Mary. Had she found a nice man to marry, she wondered, someone who wouldn't care a pin about that silly birthmark? Would he agree to let Mary send for her sister? Would he pay the steamship fare?

"'Ow I wish we'd seen Dubonnet's face," Lizzie went on, rubbing the back of one hand across her cheek and leaving a trail of soapsuds, "when 'e 'ad to explain to them 'usbands 'e'd picked out that 'e'd misplaced us."

Sarah burst out laughing, but next moment a shiver crossed her shoulders. Till that moment it hadn't occurred to her how embarrassing it must have been for Mr. Dubonnet. He was a man who refused even to have his word questioned. How he must have hated being made to look a fool in the eyes of two miners he probably considered his inferiors.

Again Sarah shivered. Right this minute he might be plotting some way to even the score.

Well, she reassured herself, even if he was, Lizzie was safe. If he was planning to get even it would have to be just with her. There was no way he could harm Lizzie now that Josh was going to marry her. As for herself, she'd just take care to keep out of his way.

Chapter 26

In the days that followed, Lizzie spent a good part of her time daydreaming — wondering where Josh was, wondering if the miners were listening to him, wondering how soon she'd see him again, wondering if he missed her.

Much of her wondering she did out loud, until Sarah was tempted to tell her to be quiet. But she held back the words. Just because *she* was determined to be independent didn't mean Lizzie was too.

Josh was spending just as much time thinking about Lizzie. Several times he'd started a letter, but mail for Barkerville had to go in the mail pouch that the Barnard Express carried. Until he reached Yale, Ashcroft or Victoria, where he could put letters into that pouch there was no point in writing. So instead he busied himself rehearsing what he'd say to the bishop when he asked permission to marry.

He'd been told that Bishop Hills liked his clergy to marry and bring their wives to their parishes with them — it showed the people they were really planning to settle. But perhaps the bishop would think him too young. He might say he and Lizzie had to wait a few years.

It was important to find the right time to speak to him, Josh decided — some time when the bishop was in a casual, relaxed mood.

His chance came just a day after he reached Victoria. An official party was being held to honor Captain McLaughlin of the *Tynemouth*, who would shortly be starting the long voyage back to England. McLaughlin was well liked and respected, and almost everyone was invited — not only the important Victoria citizens and government personnel, but all the missionaries as well.

However, Josh discovered, an invitation to the party did not guarantee a chance to speak privately with Bishop Hills. Every time he tried to approach the bishop he found him surrounded. For the better part of an hour Josh stood and waited for an opportunity to talk to him.

At last his vigil caught the attention of one of the other missionaries. "You seem very anxious to speak to Hills," the man said.

Josh was so glad to speak to someone and ask advice on how best to catch the bishop's ear, that he poured out his story without any thought for who else might be listening in the overcrowded room. Next moment, to his horror, he heard a stranger behind him call out jokingly, "Did you hear that, Dubonnet? There's a missionary here who wants to marry one of those orphan girls you brought over."

Josh looked around in dismay. Half the room was staring at him, including a rotund man with puffy side whiskers who was studying him through his monocle.

"I think you must be wrong, Tillingham," the rotund man said in a voice pitched to carry clearly. "The girls I brought over are fine for the miners, but they are scarcely the sort of women any educated cleric would care to have as a wife." His words drew a titter of amusement.

Josh felt the color creep into his cheeks. He wanted to answer back — to say that any man in the room would be lucky to have someone like Lizzie agree to marry him — but until he knew who the speaker was, he didn't dare. "Who is that?" he asked the missionary beside him in an undertone.

"A protégé of Bishop Hills'," was the reply. "His name is Dubonnet. The clergyman who recommended him as an escort for the girls is a good friend of the bishop. From the hints Dubonnet is dropping I think he is hoping for a cushy job at Hills' Boys' Collegiate School here in Victoria."

Josh was glad he'd had the sense to keep quiet. He glanced worriedly toward the bishop. Had he heard what Dubonnet had said? To his relief, Hills was facing the other way and deep in conversation. Thankful for his good luck, Josh turned to leave. Tomorrow would be time enough to speak to the bishop, he decided, and until then he wouldn't talk to anyone else about Lizzie.

He was almost at the door when a carefully casual voice spoke behind him. "Don't hurry off. We haven't been introduced. I'm Edward Dubonnet."

Reluctantly, Josh turned around. "Gillmor," he mumbled, accepting Dubonnet's outstretched hand.

"Now, about this girl you hope to marry. Is she here in Victoria?"

"No, sir." It was all he could do to be civil, for he was still smarting at the unnecessary slur Dubonnet had cast against the *Tynemouth* girls.

"In the gold fields, then?"

He didn't want to answer, but if the man who had recommended Dubonnet was a friend of the bishop, it would be a mistake to be rude. Dubonnet looked like the sort who wouldn't hesitate to complain, and if he did, Hills would never be sympathetic to a request for an early marriage. But though he managed to keep his voice civil, Josh couldn't manage *sir* a second time. "In Barkerville," he replied bluntly.

Dubonnet's face creased in a wry smile. "Then I don't think she can be one of my girls after all. Certainly, a number of *Tynemouth* girls married miners and went up to that area, but I think one husband each will be enough even for them."

At the sneer in Dubonnet's voice Josh's temper rose again. "She is a *Tynemouth* girl but she is not married," he said stiffly. No longer caring even if Dubonnet did complain about him, he turned and started toward the door.

"What is her name?" the voice pursued.

"Lizzie," Josh flung back.

"Ah." The word hung on the air.

It was so unexpected that Josh turned around. He was just in time to see what appeared to be a flush of anger on Dubonnet's face, but he could have been mistaken, for already the bland smile was back.

"Ah," he said again, letting his breath out slowly. "So that's how it was." He brushed some invisible fluff off the sleeve of his coat. "Did she tell you of all our adventures on the *Tynemouth*?" The words were innocent and he continued to concentrate on his coat sleeve.

"What do you mean, *that's how it was*?"

"Did she?" Dubonnet repeated, ignoring Josh's question.

"No, she didn't."

Dubonnet looked up. "Nothing at all?"

"Nothing."

For a moment Dubonnet continued to study Josh with a thoughtful expression, then he sighed and returned his attention to his coat. "Unfortunately, Gillmor, she will — sooner or later. Tedious as it seems, just when one thinks a job is finished, one finds it necessary to do it all over again." Slipping his monocle back into the breast pocket of his waistcoat, he moved away.

Josh gazed after him for a moment with a puzzled frown, then putting the whole thing out of his mind, returned to his lodgings. He spent the rest of the evening rehearsing what he would say to the bishop in the morning.

Promptly at ten he presented himself — to find that Dubonnet had been there before him.

"You have been badly deceived in this girl," Hills said in reply to Josh's stammered request for permission to marry Lizzie. "She is a thief and a liar. Mr. Dubonnet has just been here to give me her full history. He is a totally reliable man and was in charge of the girls on the journey from England. His word can be trusted. This girl you are planning to marry not only stole jewelry and personal possessions from the other orphan girls, but also a valuable ruby pendant from Mr. Dubonnet's sister."

For a moment, Josh was too stunned to answer.

"As Mr. Dubonnet points out, the wife of any of our missionaries is listened to and trusted as a leading citizen. If we were to allow such a disreputable girl as this to marry into our ranks, it would bring disgrace on all of us. It was to prevent such a thing happening that Mr. Dubonnet felt compelled to speak to me about her."

"Please, my lord, there must be some mistake. I know Lizzie would never —"

"There must be no further communication of any kind between you."

"But Mr. Dubonnet could have mixed her up with someone else. Lizzie would never —"

"We will not discuss this any further." As if the matter were closed, Hills moved to the window and stared outside. Then in the same stiff, ill-at-ease voice he added, "Aren't you aware that the church in England is watching what we do here with great interest? All our reputations are at stake. What hope for approbation or advancement would any of us have if word got back to England that I allowed one of our missionaries to stumble into marriage with such a woman?"

Chapter 27

When the stage arrived in Barkerville the following week it brought Lizzie a letter from Josh. She asked Sarah to read it aloud to her.

At first there were interesting, funny comments about Josh's trip and about the way he'd been received by the miners at the various centers where he'd stopped to hold services. Then he told her about the party for Captain McLaughlin and his interview with Bishop Hills. Despite his efforts to sound calm and objective, the tone of the letter changed. The hurt and pain Josh was feeling shone through clearly.

"There has to be some sort of misunderstanding," his letter finished, *"for I know what they are saying about you isn't true. If the bishop won't believe me and accept you as my*

wife, I'm going to leave the church, for I love you, Lizzie, and I want to marry you."

"'E mustn't leave the church," Lizzie said in a stricken whisper. "They need 'im. Look 'ow wonderful 'e was with Charlie."

Sarah felt as bruised and crushed inside as if she were the one to be hurt. It wasn't fair. Lizzie had been so happy — for the first time in her life things were going well — and Mr. Dubonnet had ruined everything.

She should have known that he would, Sarah told herself bitterly. She should never have assumed Lizzie was safe just because Josh wanted to marry her. They'd been lucky to slip out of the trap Mr. Dubonnet had laid for them the first time. She should have known he'd find a new way to "fix" things.

"Does 'e say anythin' else?" Lizzie managed.

With difficulty Sarah pulled her thoughts back. "Only the ending. It's signed, *Yours, Josh.*"

Lizzie held her hand out for the sheets and folded her fingers around them tightly. "If only there 'adn't bin a party fer the captain," she said in a low shaking voice. "Then maybe Dubonnet and Josh wud never 'ave met."

Sarah nodded, but she knew now that even without the party, Dubonnet would have found a way to even the score with Lizzie. If not before Josh married her, then after.

"E still 'ates us, don't 'e?"

"He's also still afraid of us."

"But why? Nobody cares any more about wot 'appened on that ship."

"He does. Remember what he said about hoping to be offered some important position? What chance would he have if we told people the truth?"

Lizzie tossed her head angrily. "Nobody wud believe us, no more than they did last time."

"They'd believe you if you were married to a clergyman. That's probably why he went to the bishop to stop the marriage.

"So wot kin we do?"

Sarah glanced away. She didn't answer.

For a minute longer Lizzie waited, then the fight drained out of her face and her shoulders sagged. "You're sayin' there's nothin' we kin do, aren't you? You're sayin' it'd be the same all over again." Her voice was slow and defeated. She looked down at the letter she was holding so tightly. "Well, I won't drag Josh down with me. Will you write 'im for me an' tell 'im 'e mustn't give up the church?"

"Lizzie . . . I . . ." Sarah wanted to tell her how she felt, but the words refused to come. Instead she nodded.

For a moment longer Lizzie clutched the letter, then she forced a smile. "I probably wudn't —" A shaky note had come into her voice. She coughed to clear it and started again. "I probably wudn't 'ave bin any good as a preacher's wife any 'ow."

Chapter 28

Each morning since Charlie's death Bill had headed out as usual for the creek bed carrying his two round panning dishes. But he didn't start out as early as he had before. He was often still at the cabin when Sarah and Lizzie arrived to begin the day's laundry. And though his daily "good morning" was cheerful and his step seemed enthusiastic as he headed down the road, Sarah knew the cheerfulness and the enthusiasm would both disappear as soon as he was out of sight.

Each evening she found an excuse to postpone leaving until after he'd come home. She asked about his day and told him funny stories about hers and Lizzie's. He laughed and joked and insisted everything was fine, but he couldn't hide the emptiness in his eyes that brought a lump to Sarah's throat.

She wondered if he was bothering to eat. She knew the bins by the stove held flour and oatmeal and biscuits, for when Charlie was still alive Bill had gone straight there each evening to fix something for both of them to eat. But he didn't do that any longer. Did he cook up something after she and Lizzie had gone? Sarah didn't know, but in the mornings there was never any sign of stored leftovers or dirty dishes.

One night when he arrived home, she had the coffee pot over the fire, some oatmeal simmering in a pot, and some dried bacon heating. She didn't leave till he started eating.

The following afternoon, she and Lizzie finished the laundry earlier than usual. That morning, Mrs. Peet had asked if one of them could come home and help with the children. Lizzie offered to go while Sarah waited for Bill.

Again she fixed something for him to eat.

His face lit with pleasure when he came in and found her waiting. "Can you stay for a while and eat with me?" he asked.

As she shared the oatmeal and coffee she found herself sharing thoughts she'd never intended to share with anyone. For some reason she wanted to tell Bill about Maud, and the searchlight, and Penelope. Fortunately, she caught herself in time. What would he think if she started confiding all her innermost thoughts?

Next moment she was glad she'd held back her confidences, for Bill seemed strangely preoccupied. Getting up from the table he moved to the stove. He stared in silence at the flames for a minute, prodded the sticks of wood, then said absentmindedly, "Some of the men are talking about leaving before winter sets in." He continued to concentrate on the fire. "Probably by mid–November. They want me to go with them."

Such a frightening hole opened up somewhere deep in Sarah's middle that she felt sick. She tried to tell herself she was being ridiculous. She'd known ever since Charlie died that one day soon Bill would decide his adventure in Barkerville was finished, and head off in search of a new one. So why did she feel so shaky and frightened?

"Do you think I should go with them?" The words were still casual, tossed over Bill's shoulder as he stood with his back turned, straightening the bits of wood piled on the floor beside the stove.

The wave of sickness in Sarah's middle grew worse. "I . . . maybe . . . if you want to," she managed, scarcely conscious of what she was saying.

"It gets cold here in the winter. Forty below temperatures are common. Last winter two of the fellows died."

Sarah nodded but she didn't answer. She couldn't trust her voice.

"If I did decide to go," Bill said carefully, still fussing with the sticks but turned slightly sideways now so he could see her face, "would you miss me?"

The new note in his voice gave Sarah a tingly

feeling inside that she'd never felt before. *Yes!* she wanted to shout. Even thinking about his leaving made her sick and trembly inside, and she wanted to tell him. But she held the words back. Maybe he wasn't serious. Several other times he'd said things that had thrown her off balance and each time it had turned out he'd been joking. If she admitted she'd miss him and it turned out he was joking this time too, she would be embarrassed.

She forced a smile. "Of course," she said in her brightest voice, taking care to make the words carefree and casual so it would sound as if she was joking too.

She expected him to laugh.

Instead an odd look crossed his face. It seemed familiar, but before Sarah could remember where she'd seen it before, he had turned away and was once again concentrating on the woodpile. "I was hoping you'd say I should try a little longer," he said in an oddly stiff tone.

For a moment Sarah was confused. She wished she could see his face. Then she understood. He wasn't even thinking of her. It was his guilt over letting Charlie down that was worrying him. Winter was coming and all his friends were leaving, and he probably wanted more than anything in the world to be able to leave with them. But he still felt guilty about Charlie. He probably thought he should try a little longer to make that strike so Charlie's family could buy their farm.

She understood how he was feeling for she'd felt the same way about Maud. But he had nothing to blame himself for, and she had to tell him so. He hadn't let Charlie down — he'd stuck by him all those months and nursed him and taken care of him and done everything he could to try to make his dream come true. "You've got to stop blaming yourself and start thinking of your own happiness," she blurted impulsively.

At that Bill turned around. A whimsical smile crept into his eyes. "I thought that was exactly what I was doing, but I guess I must have made a mess of it. Never mind. Perhaps this isn't the right time."

Now Sarah was completely off balance, and Bill must have realized it. The comfortable, brotherly smile that she was so used to returned. Putting down the bit of wood he'd been using to poke the fire, he picked up her shawl instead. "Mrs. Peet will be getting worried. You'd better be heading home." He moved to the door and opened it for her.

Sarah was halfway home before she placed that look that had crossed Bill's face after her glib "Of course." He'd worn it once before, on the day of Charlie's funeral.

They'd come back to the cabin together, and Bill had gone in first. The emptiness must have struck him, for he'd stopped in the doorway and turned back. That look had been on his face.

He hadn't been thinking about Charlie after all, she realized with a rush of guilt. He was lonely, frightened maybe, and had asked if she'd miss him because he needed to know. But instead of telling him the truth, she'd as good as told him that she wouldn't.

She had to go back and set things right. She had to explain — to make him understand. She couldn't just walk away leaving him to think she didn't care at all — not when he was still hurting so much over Charlie.

But after a dozen paces she stopped and started again toward Mrs. Peet's cabin, her cheeks burning. Perhaps he *had* been serious when he'd asked if she'd miss him, but that didn't mean it was more than a casual question. That didn't mean she should throw herself at him, which is what she'd be doing if she went back now and told him how she felt about him. He was an adventurer, he'd admitted it. Any day he might decide it was time to walk out, and when he did he'd never think of her again. He'd leave just like Poppa.

Even as that thought struck, Sarah knew it wasn't true. Bill would never be like Poppa. Bill was trustworthy. Hadn't he proved it by staying month after month with Charlie, nursing him and caring for him and struggling in that icy water trying to make a strike for him? Even now he was blaming himself that he hadn't tried harder. And he'd kept faith with her and Lizzie, too. He hadn't broken their confidence and told the others about them.

She was grateful for the gathering shadows that hid the flush she could feel creeping into her cheeks. For the first time she honestly admitted to herself how much she would miss him if he went away. Even if he did think she was throwing herself at him, she'd have to tell him.

But not tonight. It would be better to tell him tomorrow. That would be time enough. She'd talk to him first thing in the morning as soon as she and Lizzie arrived at the cabin to start the laundry.

Chapter 29

Next morning Sarah was awake soon after dawn, rehearsing what she would say — and trying to imagine Bill's response. She waited impatiently for Lizzie to waken so they could make an early start and be at the cabin well before Bill was ready to leave.

But when they came down from their sleeping loft under the roof, they found Mrs. Peet ill in bed. "Would one of you stay for a while and help with the children?" she pleaded. "Just till I'm feeling a bit better?"

"You stay," Lizzie told Sarah quickly. "I'll go do the laundry."

Sarah wanted to say no, for it would mean letting the whole day go by before she could speak to Bill — but she knew why Lizzie had spoken up so quickly. She'd seen the red rings around Lizzie's eyes each morning, and her lack of appetite at meals. So far Lizzie had managed to keep her unhappiness hidden from Mrs. Peet and the children, but only because she avoided being with them for too long at a time. If she had to stay home all day under Mrs. Peet's watchful eye, she'd give herself away for certain.

So Sarah let Lizzie go off alone. But the hours dragged, particularly after it occurred to her that Bill might think she'd stayed home on purpose to avoid him.

By mid-afternoon, however, Mrs. Peet was feeling better. "Maybe you should go and see if Lizzie needs help finishing up," she suggested.

Eagerly, Sarah agreed. As she hurried the half mile to the cabin she rehearsed again what she would say. She hoped she'd get there before Bill got home, so she could fix something for his supper and do her explaining while he ate.

To her relief, she was in time. She saw no sign of Bill's high rubber gumboots or his panning dishes outside the door as she approached the cabin. But there was no sign of Lizzie outside at the washtub either, which was odd. Lizzie couldn't have finished and gone home, or Sarah would have seen her on the path. Perhaps she was inside cleaning up the cabin, Sarah decided, moving toward the door.

But after only half a dozen paces she stopped, for through the paneless window she could see Lizzie. She wasn't tidying up. She was sitting on the cabin's only wooden chair, sobbing.

Sarah's heart caught.

Everything was her fault. If only there were some way she could undo that evening on the *Tynemouth*. If only she hadn't insisted that Lizzie pick those locks, or at least had found the courage to share the blame. Instead, she'd thought only of herself.

She should have known running away wouldn't solve anything. She should have known Mr. Dubonnet would find a way to take his revenge. But why couldn't he have taken it against her? Why did he have to pick on Lizzie, just when she had a chance for happiness?

Filled with self-reproach, Sarah turned and went away again as quietly as she'd come.

When she arrived back at the house she didn't go in. Instead, she continued along the deserted path that circled the cemetery, determined to get her feelings back under control before encountering Mrs. Peet — who would otherwise guess at once that something was wrong. But instead of growing calmer, she grew more and more agitated, for there was nothing she could do to change any of what had happened.

Except there was, she realized.

There *was* something she could do! She could publicly denounce Dubonnet as a thief and a liar. She could tell the truth about what had happened on the *Tynemouth* — how Dubonnet framed Lizzie so she wouldn't be able to speak out against him.

True, to do so meant coming out of hiding. And if Dubonnet denied her charges and was listened to, then she'd have put Lizzie and herself back in his power for no purpose. But though no one else might listen, she knew *Josh* would. And she owed Lizzie that much at least. Though he'd insisted in his letter that he had total faith in her, if Dubonnet kept repeating his lies, Josh might have private dark moments when he had twinges of doubt. But if Sarah spoke up, even though Josh and Lizzie would probably never able to marry, still he'd know for sure for the rest of his life that Lizzie was innocent. That much, at least, Sarah could do to make up.

Then she remembered Bill, and her courage weakened. Of course she wasn't going to become dependent on him — but he was her friend and she didn't want to give that up. She had a right to happiness too. She had a right to —

Even as that thought came into her mind she knew it wasn't true. Happiness had to be earned. Instead of earning hers, she'd thrown it away by her cowardice and selfishness that morning on the *Tynemouth*. If she'd spoken up at the very beginning Captain McLaughlin might have listened.

Once more she circled the cemetery, then slowly returned home. Up in the tiny partition under the roof where she and Lizzie slept, she took one of the few remaining sheets of Maud's writing paper from her worn carpetbag and sat down to write a letter. When it was finished to her satisfaction, she folded it carefully and tucked it back in the carpetbag. Then she reached under her mattress for the small tin box that was hidden there.

Every evening since she and Lizzie had started their laundry business she'd paid Mrs. Peet from the day's earnings, then put anything that was left over into that box. Over the weeks the amount of money had grown. Now, emptying it out onto the bed, she counted the coins. Moments later she left the house.

This time when she returned, Lizzie was waiting.

"Where 'ave you bin?" Lizzie's cheery tone belied the redness around her eyes. "I thought you wos to stay 'ome an' look after all them children."

"I did. But I had an errand to do." Sarah held out what she'd bought.

"Tickets fer the stage? To go where?"

"Victoria."

It was as if the sun had come out somewhere inside Lizzie's eyes. "'As Josh sent for me? Is that why you got the tickets?"

Sarah's heart twisted. She shook her head. "Josh doesn't know anything about it. But we can't let Mr. Dubonnet spread lies about you any longer. We've got to stand up to him and try to make people listen to the truth."

The life faded from Lizzie's face. "Wot's the point? It won't work."

"How do you know?"

"Cos it didn't work the last time."

"This time is more important."

Lizzie frowned. "Why?"

"Because of Josh."

For a long moment Lizzie continued to frown, then a tiny glimmer of life crept back into her green eyes. "D'you mean you think Josh'll 'ear if we try to tell the truth?"

"Of course he'll hear."

For a minute Lizzie was silent, staring into the middle distance at something Sarah couldn't see, then she said softly, "No matter wot 'appens afterward, I want Josh to know for absolute certain that I wosn't no thief." The glimmer of life in her eyes started to build. "'Ow soon d'we go?"

"On the stage tomorrow morning." As she spoke Sarah turned away, for while Lizzie's dreams had been reborn, her own had turned into empty air. There was to be no adventure after all, in spite of all her brave talk. There was to be no more friendship with Bill. She didn't know why that seemed so important, but it did. First thing tomorrow she would be leaving, and she'd never see him again.

The lost empty feeling she'd experienced the night before was nothing compared with what swept over her now. Not only would Bill think she didn't care enough about him to miss him, he'd think she didn't care enough even to come and say goodbye.

As the hours of the night crept by, Sarah counted each one. Long before morning, she knew she couldn't let Bill learn from someone else that she had gone away. She had to tell him herself. If she got up as soon as it was light she could stop by his cabin for a minute and still be back in time for the stage.

Soon after dawn, she was awake. She slipped out of bed without waking Lizzie, dressed quietly, then hurried the familiar half mile to Bill's cabin. She'd tell him she was leaving, she decided, but she wouldn't say anything about why. If she did, she'd end up admitting how she'd failed Lizzie on the *Tynemouth* — and then he'd despise her. She'd tell him how much she'd miss him, and how much she'd enjoyed being friends, then wish him good luck and hurry away before he could ask any questions.

Bill opened the door to her knock. A smile sprang to his eyes. "I was afraid when you didn't come yesterday that I must have offended you," he said softly, the same warm note in his voice that had shaken her off balance two evenings before.

Sarah's well rehearsed speech was forgotten. "I wanted to come yesterday but Mrs. Peet was sick and I had to stay to help her," she said in a rush. "Then when I could finally get away, it was too late."

"Too late?" Bill's voice was carefully non-committal.

"I wanted to explain that I'd only been pretending I wouldn't miss you, only Lizzie was crying and I knew I had to try to make things right." The words continued to pour out in a disorganized stream. "But I couldn't leave without saying goodbye, so I've come this morning." She'd run out of words.

While she'd been talking, Bill had led her into the cabin and closed the door. Now he poured a cup of tea from the pot he had steeping on the stove, and put it into her hands. Still smiling he said softly, "Do you think we could start again? Why was Lizzie crying, why is it too late, where are you going that you need to say goodbye, and . . ." a husky note crept into his voice, "would you really miss me if I went away?"

In spite of all her resolutions, Sarah found herself telling him about the masquerade, and picking the locks, and letting Lizzie take all the blame. "When I finally had the courage to tell the truth, no one would listen." She was avoiding Bill's eyes now, for fear she'd read disgust in them. "But Mr. Dubonnet has started spreading lies about Lizzie all over again, and this time I'm going to try to stop him."

"Will you be coming back?"

"I don't know." The words were scarcely more than a whisper and the tea she was holding almost spilled. "People may not believe us this time either. If they don't," her voice dropped even lower, "Mr. Dubonnet will fix it so Lizzie and I can never bother him again."

For a moment Bill was silent. Then, in an entirely different voice, he said, "You haven't answered the last part of my question."

Sarah looked up in confusion. "Pardon?"

He was smiling down at her in a way that started her heart doing funny things all over again. "Would you really miss me if I went away? I think I should know, if I'm going to wait for you."

Sarah's glance flew to his face. What she read there brought the blood rushing to her cheeks. "Yes, oh yes," she whispered. Then, knowing if she didn't leave right then she'd forget all about her promise to Lizzie, she turned and hurried out of the cabin.

Chapter 30

The Barnard Express stage took four days to reach Ashcroft, and four more to reach Yale. There the passengers got on another coach that connected with the ferry that took them over to Victoria.

With every mile, Sarah's loneliness and heartache grew. She knew how slim the chances were that they could tackle Mr. Dubonnet and win — how little hope there was that she would ever see Bill again. But she tried to hide her feelings, for Lizzie was bubbling with excitement.

"Now wot?" Lizzie said when they finally reached the Victoria stagecoach depot.

"Get a place to stay tonight," Sarah replied, checking the small sum of money they still had left, "then we're going to talk to Judge Begbie."

"'Oo?"

"The person Mrs. Peet told me we should go to for legal advice." Avoiding Lizzie's eyes and keeping her voice casual Sarah added, "But first we've got to find Captain McLaughlin and talk to him."

"Wot good will that do." Lizzie's voice was acid. The words were a statement, not a question.

Silently, Sarah couldn't help but agree. The captain had refused to stand up for them before. He'd very likely refuse again. Still, they had to ask for his help because he was their only chance. Unless they had some well known adult to support their story Judge Begbie would never believe them.

Next morning they were at the stage office when it opened to ask directions. The man in charge told them where the captain was staying, but when they asked for directions to reach the judge's chambers he shook his head. "Judge Begbie's office is in New Westminster," he told them apologetically.

For a minute Sarah was too stunned to take it in, then deep inside she felt shaky and frightened. It was the end of everything. Why hadn't she thought to ask Mrs. Peet where Judge Begbie had his office? Why had she assumed it would be in Victoria? It would have been hard enough to convince the captain to speak on their behalf if the judge's chambers had been close by, but he'd never agree to do so if it meant traveling all that way.

"The boat trip from here to New Westminster takes most of the day," the clerk's voice broke through Sarah's distress. "But if you catch the one leaving in about half an hour you should be there before the judge's office closes this afternoon."

Sarah could feel Lizzie watching her. She wanted to say no, they weren't going — that they weren't trying any more — that everything was too difficult. She wanted to rip up the letter in her bag for Captain McLaughlin, for she knew he'd never travel all that distance just to support them. She wanted to go home before it was too late. Lizzie would undertand.

But the gleam of hope in Lizzie's eyes was impossible to ignore. She'd failed Lizzie before. She wasn't going to fail her again, even if it did mean the end of their adventure. Right from the start all she'd ever hoped to do was tell the truth so Josh would hear. Even without Captain McLaughlin she could still do that. And maybe — just maybe — the captain *would* come.

Opening her carpetbag, Sarah took out the letter she'd written so carefully in the tiny upper sleeping area at Mrs. Peet's house. "Is there some place where I can leave this letter for Captain McLaughlin?" she asked.

"I'll see that he gets it." The clerk held out his hand.

Sarah hesitated. She'd been counting on talking to the captain privately before asking him to speak in their support in front of Judge

Begbie. Otherwise, how could she be sure what he might say? What if he agreed to come, then played down her accusations? Or worse, what if he threw his support behind Dubonnet? But he was the only hope they had. Hesitantly she handed over her letter. "When you see him, will you tell him we are on our way to New Westminster to talk to Judge Begbie?"

The clerk nodded.

It was almost four when the boat docked at New Westminster harbor. At four-thirty, Sarah and Lizzie were being admitted to Judge Begbie's chambers.

Sarah's first reaction was surprise that such a famous man had such a small, unprepossessing office. Then the room was forgotten as she looked at the man himself.

The stern, piercing eyes gazing back at her were so frightening that for a moment she couldn't find any words at all. Then, knowing if she didn't speak up he might ask them to leave, she said quietly, "I'm sorry for bursting in on you this way. I know you must have far more important people to worry about — but Lizzie and I have no one else to turn to."

Perhaps it was her youth, or the quiet, composed tone of her voice, or her appeal for his help — whatever the reason, the piercing gaze softened.

"We came with the girls on the *Tynemouth*," Sarah went on quickly. Then in simple concise phrases, she told him what had happened — how Mr. Dubonnet had stolen food and personal possessions from the girls in his charge — how Lizzie had found out — how Dubonnet had planted a valuable pendant in Lizzie's bunk to make it look as if she was the thief. "Now one of the missionaries wants to marry her, only the bishop won't let him because he thinks she's a thief and a liar."

At the first mention of Dubonnet's name Begbie frowned, but he waited till Sarah had finished before saying brusquely, "I know Mr. Dubonnet. This is a serious accusation. Have you a witness who will corroborate your story?"

Sarah nodded. She told him about Captain McLaughlin and the letter she had left for him. "Only he's in Victoria," she added.

For a moment Begbie seemed to be deliberating. Then he said evenly, "For everyone's sake this matter must be looked into and settled, particularly if, as I have been told, Dubonnet has ambitions to teach school or enter the ministry. I'll get word both to him and to McLaughlin asking them to come to an informal meeting here in my chambers. You two girls will of course be here also. Let's say the day after tomorrow, to allow time for the men to travel."

At his reference to Dubonnet, Sarah must have looked alarmed, for in a softer tone Begbie added, "It is only fair that you should make your accusations in front of Mr. Dubonnet, so he can defend himself. And you will have the captain to support you."

But when the interminable wait was over and the time for the scheduled meeting had arrived, only Dubonnet was waiting to face Sarah and Lizzie in the judge's chambers. For an hour longer Begbie waited, then he said they would have to proceed without the captain.

They had lost. Till that moment, Sarah hadn't admitted even to herself how much she was counting on the captain's support. True, she had no way of knowing to what extent he might have backed up their story, but his presence alone would have given their words some credibility. Now that he had ignored their appeal they had no chance of being believed. Mr. Dubonnet would simply accuse them of lying, then make sure they could never speak out against him again.

Perhaps there was still time to pretend the whole thing had been a mistake! It wasn't too late. If they said nothing — if they took back their accusations and put themselves in the judge's hands, surely he'd look after them and see that Dubonnet couldn't —

Sarah pushed the thought away. She'd failed Lizzie before. She wasn't going to fail her again — no matter what Dubonnet might do to her and Lizzie afterward. Raising her head and looking straight at Judge Begbie she repeated the story she had told him two days earlier.

It was as if the clock had been turned back. The only difference was that they were in the judge's chambers, not on a ship. As Sarah repeated her accusation Dubonnet's expression changed from annoyance to amusement.

When at last Sarah finished, Dubonnet got

lazily to his feet. "As I'm sure you realize, your Lordship, this is all sheer fabrication." He looked and sounded unruffled, but as he glanced over at Sarah she caught the icy hardness at the back of his eyes. "However, I know your Lordship will be the first to agree that this sort of thing is damaging to a man's reputation. I'd be grateful, therefore, if you would see that both these girls are put some place where they cannot repeat such slander."

Begbie continued to sit in watchful silence.

"Particularly that one." Dubonnet pointed at Lizzie. "She is a proven thief and liar." Disgust rang in his tone. "One wonders who her next victim might be."

Sarah didn't dare look at Lizzie, for she knew if she did she'd burst into tears. It had all been for nothing. No word of what had been said at this private meeting would get out to Josh or to anyone else. Why hadn't she left well enough alone? Right this minute they could still be in Barkerville. She and Bill —

If she thought about Bill she knew she'd cry, and for Lizzie's sake she had to be strong. Whatever happened, she was determined never to give Dubonnet the satisfaction of knowing how much he was hurting them.

For the past few moments, Sarah had been vaguely aware of someone at the office door, but she'd been too busy with her own thoughts to pay attention. Now, however, a voice spoke clearly. "Excuse me, your Lordship, for being late. May I come in?"

Sarah's heart rose with sudden hope and excitement for it was Captain McLaughlin.

Begbie nodded, thanked him for coming, indicated a vacant chair, waited till he was settled, then asked him to describe what had happened on board the *Tynemouth*. He did so in words that paralleled almost exactly the ones Sarah had used.

"The man is lying!" Dubonnet blustered, but his complacency was noticeably shaken.

Judge Begbie continued to watch McLaughlin, his face expressionless. "Unfortunatley, one man's word against another is inconclusive unless there are supporting witnesses."

"The girls' testimony supports my word."

"But they are minors."

"Then, if you will allow me, your Lordship, I'd like to present another witness who is not a minor."

Next moment a lady dressed all in stunning pink came into the room.

"I was afraid you hadn't got my letter, or that you weren't going to come," Sarah told the captain shyly as they were leaving the judge's chambers.

He glanced from Sarah to Lizzie, then back again. In a voice blunt with self–criticism he admitted, "I owe you both an apology for the way I acted that day on board ship. I've spent many weeks regretting my cowardice." A wry smile pulled at the corners of his lips. "However, my delay in coming to New Westminster was not caused by the same cowardice. I had an idea I might need a corroborating voice, and I had difficulty locating her." He glanced sideways at Bea. In an even drier voice he added, "She was working, and I wasn't allowed to interrupt."

Bea burst out laughing.

"Will somebody write Josh fer me, an' tell 'im I'm no thief?" Lizzie asked shyly when the laughter subsided. A rosy flush crept into her cheeks. "'Is address is on this." Reaching into her pocket, she took out the well-thumbed letter she had carried with her everywhere.

"I'll do better than write," McLaughlin offered. "I'll speak to him in person and explain."

Lizzie beamed. "Soon?"

"As soon as we all get back to Victoria, for I'm taking you two with me."

Lizzie beamed even more brightly.

"Someone should also speak to Bishop Hills," Bea suggested.

"Begbie's sure to do that," McLaughlin replied. "He'll want Hills to know that Dubonnet is hardly the sort of man the church will want as a minister or headmaster."

"But either you or I should also speak to the bishop," Bea insisted. "He must be told the whole story, not just its conclusion. Otherwise he might still oppose the marriage."

"Would *you* speak to him?" Sarah asked.

For a moment that idea seemed to amuse Bea, then she forced the corners of her mouth to behave. "On second thought it might be better if the captain attended to that as well," she said innocently, adjusting the lace on the sleeve of her gown. "My calling on the bishop might result in his having to make some rather embarrassing explanations to his clergy."

McLaughlin chuckled delightedly. "You're right. I'll attend to it." He turned to Sarah. "It took courage to do what you did, my dear."

"She has Penelope," Bea said simply as if that explained everything. She turned to Sarah and added quietly, "Don't ever grow too old for her."

"That wos it!" Lizzie exclaimed. "That's wot you said that day on the ship. I couldn't remember!"

For a moment longer Bea stood smiling at them, then with a half wave, she turned and moved away. She didn't look back.

The wedding, with Bishop Hills' approval, was held two days later in Victoria.

"You'll make a wonderful preacher's wife," Sarah told Lizzie softly.

Lizzie beamed. "Now we'll fix you up. Let's go right now an' talk to that library man wot Mr. Bowron told you about."

Sarah shook her head.

"But you said workin' in a library wos what you always dreamed of."

"I know. But I've changed my mind."

"Wot are you gonna do instead?"

"Finish my adventure," Sarah said with a soft, private smile.

"Wot?" Lizzie sounded confused.

Sarah didn't explain, but she knew he'd still be there, for he'd said he'd wait and she trusted him.

Tomorrow, she'd start back. Ten days from tomorrow she'd be in Barkerville.

The end